After he'd seen Amelia to the door, and said goodnight, he concentrated on getting his daughter settled.

While he sat by her bed, stroking her blonde curls, he thought about Amelia and how tempting it had been to simply walk into the house, cross to her side and kiss her.

For the past two days Amelia had been here, caring for his daughter, and somehow she'd put her stamp on the place. Nothing had outwardly changed, but when he walked into the kitchen he could smell her perfume. When he looked at Yolanda's room he pictured Amelia and his daughter, side by side, playing dolls. Thoughts of her, visions of her, were all around his house—and it felt...right.

A&E DRAMA
Drama in the Emergency Room

Blood pressure is high and pulses are racing
in these fast-paced dramatic stories from
Mills & Boon® Medical Romance™.
They'll move a mountain to save a life
in an emergency, be they the crash team,
emergency doctors, or paramedics. There
are lots of critical engagements amongst the
high tensions and emotional passions in these
exciting stories of lives and loves at risk!

THE EMERGENCY DOCTOR'S DAUGHTER

BY
LUCY CLARK

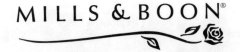

MILLS & BOON®

First published in Great Britain 2007
Harlequin Mills & Boon Limited,
Eton House, 18-24 Paradise Road, Richmond, Surrey TW9 1SR

© Lucy Clark 2007

ISBN-13: 978 0 263 19587 3
ISBN-10:   0 263 19587 2

Set in Times Roman 10½ on 12½ pt
07-0207-46665

Printed and bound in Great Britain
by Antony Rowe Ltd, Chippenham, Wiltshire

Lucy Clark began writing romance in her early teens, and immediately knew she'd found her 'calling' in life. After working as a secretary in a busy teaching hospital, she turned her hand to writing medical romance. She currently lives in South Australia, with her husband and two children. Lucy largely credits her writing success to the support of her husband, family and friends.

Recent titles by the same author:

THE SURGEON'S COURAGEOUS BRIDE
IN HIS SPECIAL CARE
A KNIGHT TO HOLD ON TO

To Karen—thanks for always being there
for a lovely long phone chat.
They're much appreciated.
Ps 18:2

CHAPTER ONE

'OK. THAT'S finished.' Amelia stood and closed the case notes she'd just finished writing up. 'I'm going to have my lunch-break now,' she told Rosie Jefferson, the accident and emergency triage sister.

'Go.' Rosie nodded. 'Tina's still around, isn't she?'

'Cubicle three, I think.'

'All right. See you back here in half an hour, if not before,' Rosie teased, and Amelia groaned.

'I order no emergencies for at least the next hour or two.'

'Is that when your shift ends?'

'About then.' Amelia smiled and headed out of the A and E department towards the cafeteria, pleased she'd managed to remember the way rather than getting lost as she'd done the other day. The cafeteria was busy, crowded with the usual mix of hospital staff, patients and their families. Glenelg General Hospital wasn't as big as some of the ones she'd worked in over the years and was definitely smaller than her hospital back home in England where she'd undertaken most of her medical training. Still, it was a nice place to work, close to the beach and the apartment she'd found for her three-month stint here.

Amelia browsed the food on offer, picking up a yoghurt and trying to decide what else she wanted to eat. An elderly woman brushed passed her, jostling her shoulder, and the tub of yoghurt slipped out of her hand.

'Sorry,' the woman called, and Amelia saw the frantic look on her face before she bent to pick up the—thankfully—unopened tub. She rubbed her shoulder and continued looking, deciding on a not-too-heavy salad roll.

Making her way back towards the A and E tearoom, Amelia heard a strange noise and stopped, listening carefully. It sounded as though someone was crying. She turned and headed down a small side corridor, which had a flickering fluorescent light casting a start-stop eerie glow.

The crying came again and she homed in on the sound, stunned to find a little girl pressed up against the wall, hugging her knees as she watched Amelia's approach with wide, scared eyes. The poor darling looked to be no more than about three years old. She had a mass of blonde ringlets which framed her heart-shaped face.

'Hello, sweetheart,' Amelia said softly. 'Are you all right?' She crossed to the girl's side and crouched down. 'Are you all right, darling? Are you hurt?'

The little girl's bottom lip began to wobble again and Amelia's heart wrenched at the sight. 'Oh, don't cry, sweetheart. It's all right. I'm a doctor.' She pointed to the stethoscope around her neck as proof. 'I can help you.'

'You doctor?' the girl hiccuped.

'That's right. Are you hurt?'

'No.'

'Are you lost?'

She nodded.

'You poor darling. You must be so scared. Would you like me to help you find your mummy?'

'Daddy,' the girl said.

'You've lost your daddy?'

The bottom lip wobbled again and a few more tears were squeezed out as she nodded.

'It's all right, it's all right.' Amelia reassured her as best she could. 'Why don't we find your daddy?' She shifted her food into one hand and held out the other to the scared girl. 'We can find him together, all right?'

The girl nodded again and put her hand into Amelia's. 'My name is Amelia. Can you say that? It's a bit of a tricky name.'

'Meel-ya,' the girl repeated.

'Well. It's obviously not tricky for you, is it? You must be very clever.'

'Yes.' The tears had dried but the way she was gripping Amelia's hand showed she was still a little scared.

'What's your name?' Amelia asked.

'*Lan*-da.'

'My, that's a pretty name and perfect for a pretty girl. Come on. Let's go see if we can find your daddy. Is Daddy sick?'

'No.'

'Daddy's not sick in a bed?'

'No.'

'Is he hurt?'

'Yes. He hurt his hand.'

'Oh. Poor Daddy.'

'I pix.'

Amelia smiled, not sure she understood what the child was saying. If her father had a sore hand, chances were he was in A and E, being treated. They walked back the way Amelia had come but a moment later a man burst from the stairwell, his gaze frantic as he searched around him.

He was wearing a pair of tatty denim jeans, a grey T-shirt with a casual checked shirt over the top, hanging open. He had work boots on, boots which were splattered with paint, as, she realised, were his clothes. He also had an old bandage around his hand, most of which was hanging off.

He turned to look at them and as Amelia watched the instant relief wash over his face, she knew they'd found Landa's father. The child broke free from Amelia and ran towards him.

'Daddy!' she squealed, and he scooped her up into his arms, hugging her so tight Amelia wondered whether the child could breathe.

'Where did you go? Daddy was so worried,' he said, and although his words were chastising, it didn't outweigh the total happiness Amelia could see. She waited a moment then the painter came towards her, shifting his daughter to his hip, holding her with his bandaged hand. It obviously didn't hurt that much.

'Thank you. Thank you so much,' he said, and smiled. The action changed his face, softening his features which had looked so drawn and anxious before. His brown eyes, so rich and deep, were filled with relief and thanks. He raked his free hand through his thick dark hair, his lips slowly starting to relax from the smile.

He had a perfectly straight nose and a slightly chiselled jaw. His shoulders were broad, giving him an air of confidence that fitted him perfectly. In fact, he seemed to radiate that rebel-without-a-cause attitude that said he didn't care what anyone thought of him.

The world seemed to have slowed down as Amelia took in the rest of his features at a glance and she began to feel a strange stirring in the pit of her stomach such as she'd never experienced before. The stirring of anticipation and excitement, that something amazing was about to happen, which was ridiculous because this man was not only a patient here in the hospital but also probably had a wife and, no doubt, a gaggle of other little blonde-haired girls at home.

He definitely had a quality about him, one that had brought out a reaction in her—something totally foreign to her. She'd never been instantly attracted to anyone in her life.

He held out his hand and she accepted it, working hard at ignoring the way the simplest touch of his skin against hers was enough to ignite her entire body. She withdrew her hand instantly.

'Thank you,' he said again. 'She got away from my housekeeper.' He looked at his daughter. 'Mrs D.'s been very worried, pumpkin. She's been looking everywhere for you.' Landa merely buried her face into his neck and his grip on her tightened.

'I think she's had quite a fright herself,' Amelia said. 'But everyone's reunited now. I don't think she'll go wandering off any time soon.' She smiled and sucked in a breath, knowing she should move, that she should leave, but for some reason her legs simply weren't obeying the commands her brain was sending.

'Let's hope not,' the painter said, and tickled his daughter's tummy. The child lifted her head, a little giggle escaping her lips. Both adults smiled and Amelia felt envy fill her heart at the way both man and child seemed to be so well connected. It was a pretty picture.

'Well…I'd better get back.'

The painter nodded, then pointed to the food in her hand. 'Sorry for taking up your break time.'

She waved his words away. 'I'm used to it.' She looked to Landa. 'You take care now, and keep Daddy safe.'

'Yes.' The girl nodded enthusiastically, ringlets bobbing every which way. 'Bye, Meel-ya.'

'Goodbye, sweetheart.' Amelia held out her hand and Landa took it, giving it a shake before letting go. As Amelia walked away she swallowed over the lump that had risen in her throat, wondering how she was ever going to get her salad roll past it. How she'd love to have a child like Landa. That man and his wife were lucky indeed.

She sighed and shook her head as she entered the tearoom, switching on the television in need of something to distract her thoughts.

'Terrific. A medical drama,' she groaned, but nevertheless sat to watch it. Twenty minutes later, she'd had enough of the absolute tripe on the screen, as a perfectly made-up patient in high heels and a very low-cut hospital gown fluttered her eyelids at a very handsome young doctor, who was apparently the only one who could save her life.

'Oh, for crying out loud!' Amelia looked around for something to throw at the television but, apart from throwing her spoon, which she was still using to eat her yoghurt, she couldn't find anything. The door to the A and E tearoom opened and her fellow registrar, Tina, walked in.

'Are you watching that hospital soap garbage again?' She laughed at Amelia as she headed to the urn, helping herself to coffee.

'Obviously. I need something to give a lift to my day.'

'And this is it? Honey, you're getting in a rut.'

'I know.' Amelia's pager sounded and then Tina's did as well. They checked the details and found they were both the same.

'There's something to get you out of the rut,' Tina grumbled, and flicked her blonde hair over her shoulder, looking longingly at her drink. 'Why do they insist on paging both of us?' They'd been at work since early yesterday evening thanks to a big emergency and now, being close to three o'clock on a Friday afternoon, they were more than ready to leave.

'I'll take it,' Amelia said. 'You have your break. I'll page you if you're needed.' She stood and headed over to the television.

'You may as well leave it on,' Tina said, as she sat in the seat Amelia had just vacated. 'I need something to laugh at. Plus, those actors are pure eye-candy.'

Amelia shrugged. 'I guess so.' She put her yoghurt container in the bin and washed her spoon.

'Oh, come on. You can't tell me that you don't think these guys are cute?'

Amelia smiled and glanced at the TV once more. 'Maybe.' And for some reason the painter she'd met almost half an hour ago came to mind. He was pure eye-candy and she'd definitely been attracted. Of course, she would only admit it to Tina, the two having been friends for many years. Amelia had first met Tina when the blonde registrar had come to England for part of her A and E training course and it had been Tina who, in turn, had helped set up Amelia's last three-month placement here at Glenelg General Hospital in Adelaide, Australia. Amelia had spent the previous three months in Brisbane and once she'd finished her stint here, she could return to the UK, take her final exams and become a qualified A and E specialist.

That was definitely something to look forward to and she didn't need any distractions, especially not where good-looking men were concerned. The actors on the tube posed no threat to her well-ordered life and that was the way she planned to keep it. All of those characters were just figments of some writer's imagination, with the wardrobe and make-up departments making the actors look the attractive studs they were supposed to be. Until she'd met Landa's father, Amelia had wondered whether there really were men that attractive out there in the world...*real* men who weren't models or actors and who wanted to stay home and play happy families.

Mr Sexy-Painter had certainly been that type and she was glad he'd been able to change her perception. Was he still in A and E? Had Tina fixed up his hand? She decided not to say anything as it was much better for her to put him right out of her mind.

'I'll see you later, Tina. Oh, by the way, are we still on for our girls' day tomorrow?'

'Yes. If we meet at ten, we can do some shopping and then have lunch.'

'*Really* looking forward to it.' She smiled before heading to the accident and emergency nurses' station. 'Hi, Rosie, I'm here,' she said to the triage sister. 'What's up?'

'Ambulance is just about to arrive. Two teenagers were found in the back of a school room, unconscious.'

'Drugs?

'Alcohol. Vodka.'

Amelia sighed and shook her head. 'Ages?'

Rosie consulted her notes. 'Both sixteen.'

'OK. We'll set up for gastric lavage in both treatment rooms one and two.'

'Sure. Oh, and, Amelia, the other reason I paged you?'

'Yes?' Amelia sighed, wondering what else she had

to deal with. She just wanted to get these kids sorted out and go home.

Rosie leaned in closer and said in a stage whisper, 'I heard you haven't met Harrison yet.'

'The A and E director? No. He was away when I arrived last week.'

'Well, he's back.'

'What? Where?' Amelia looked around, searching for a new, unfamiliar face. There was a woman with a stethoscope around her neck, talking to a mother who was holding a toddler. Wrong gender—obviously not him.

Then her gaze fell on Mr Sexy-Painter himself. A tingle began in her toes and started to work its way up to engulf her entire body. He was still here and he still had that tatty bandage on his hand. His daughter, however, wasn't with him as he spoke to one of the nurses. The nurse in question was smiling brightly.

'That's him.' Rosie angled her head. 'The one with the bandaged hand.'

Amelia's eyebrows shot up in surprise. 'The se—um...painter?' She couldn't believe she'd almost said sexy painter! What was wrong with her today? She needed to get herself together and focus, especially if what Rosie was saying was true. Mr Sexy-Painter was really *Dr* Sexy-Painter and her *boss*.

'Yes.'

Just then, he turned and looked her way and the previous tingling that had flooded her body started exploding like fireworks. Amelia found it impossible to look away as he excused himself from the nurse and began walking towards her with firm strides, his gaze never faltering from hers.

Within an instant, he was standing in front of her. 'Dr Watson, I presume,' he said with a slight grin.

His deep voice washed over her and for a split second she couldn't breathe. Then he blinked and it was as though she'd been released from whatever had been holding her so enthralled. Amelia glanced away and sighed, saying with forced joviality, 'Haven't heard that one before.'

'Sorry. Couldn't resist.' His smile reached his eyes and she could feel herself becoming captivated once more.

'Try.'

He watched her for a moment before nodding slowly. 'So, we meet again.'

'We do.'

'I'm Harrison. Harrison Stapleton, director.'

Amelia nodded. 'A face to the name.' She jerked back, desperate to get herself under control. 'Uh…where's your daughter?' she asked. 'Somewhere safe, I hope.'

Harrison's smile was as sexy as it had been the first time she'd seen it. 'Yes. My housekeeper has taken her home. She said they both needed to lie down.' He shook his head. 'Poor Mrs D. She'd taken Yolanda to the cafeteria to get something to eat, was standing in line to pay and turned around to discover Yolanda had wandered off again.'

Amelia thought back to the woman who'd jostled her. It all added up. 'Does Yolanda often wander off?'

'Yes. Where do you think all these grey hairs have come from?' He pointed to his temples. Amelia smiled. She liked the flecks of grey. It made him look more distinguished.

'It must be a constant worry to you.'

'It is but we're working on it. It's trying to get Yolanda to be conscious of when she's actually starting to wander, that's the difficult part.'

Amelia was intrigued. From the way Harrison spoke, she got the feeling there was something wrong with Yolanda. The girl's features showed no physical abnormality but that didn't mean to say there wasn't something else going on inside the little girl's mind. Anyway, it was really none of her business. 'Well, I'm glad she's safe.'

'You and me both.' He raised a hand to his heart and patted it, leaning in a little closer, as though he was about to take her into his confidence. Amelia automatically took a step backwards, his spicy scent teasing her senses. She could feel the warmth from his body and was surprised the way her own body responded to that heat. She met his gaze as he spoke. 'I felt as though I aged about fifty years in five minutes.'

'You looked it.' She shifted, resisting the urge to place a hand to her cheek to see if she really was blushing due to his nearness. It was ridiculous.

Harrison eased back, laughing at her words. 'How very complimentary of you, Dr Watson. Anyway, sorry I wasn't here when you started work last week.'

'It's fine. I've settled in. Besides, I was told you were at a conference.'

'I was. I would rather have been here, though.'

'Didn't enjoy it? I heard it was on the Gold Coast. That's a nice enough area.'

Harrison smiled. 'It was. I'm just not one for sitting around listening to speakers when I could be out enjoying myself.'

'Then it would have been called a holiday, not a conference.'

He chuckled. 'Good point.'

Amelia found she liked the sound as it washed over her and realised it was difficult to keep her focus with him so near. She was always focused. What was wrong with her? She had her goals and a little flirtation with her boss wasn't going to deter her…not that he was really flirting with her or anything. At least, she didn't think he was. 'Um…and your hand?' She pointed to the bandage. 'You hurt yourself while you were away?'

Harrison glanced down as though he'd forgotten. 'Oh. The hand. No. I did that this morning. I was opening a tin of paint and slipped. It's not damaged.'

'Really? Looks as though you need a new bandage on it.'

Harrison frowned at the bandage and turned his hand over to survey the handiwork. 'I think it looks quite good. A real professional job. The cutest little nurse did it for me.' His smile was one of pleasure and pride and Amelia tried hard not to roll her eyes.

'I have no doubt.'

Harrison watched her face, noting that she didn't seem impressed with his words. He smiled. 'You're jumping to conclusions.'

'Well, have you given me any reason not to jump?'

His smile was almost infuriating. 'No. Probably not.' Harrison continued to watch his new registrar's expressions, seeing her impatience and annoyance wash over her. She wasn't what he'd call classically pretty but her blue eyes had a certain fire in them he appreciated. Her auburn hair was cut short in a style that wouldn't require her to do much with it when she woke up. She was dressed in a business skirt and shirt, neat and tidy, and she was about five feet six inches, her body in proportion to her height. She wore plain gold earrings and a stethoscope around her neck.

'I guess we'd better get ready,' Harrison continued after a moment.

'For?' Amelia raised her eyebrows, trying to figure out what he was talking about. He'd given her a strange look before he'd spoken, a look that had seemed to say he was satisfied with what he saw. Amazingly, it made her feel kind of pleased when in reality she thought she should have been offended by his brief perusal.

'Emergency. Ambulance arriving. Teenagers who've drunk too much alcohol? Ring any bells?'

'Yes, Dr Stapleton, it does. Thank you for the reminder. *I'll* go now and get ready. No doubt you need to go and check on your daughter or catch up on paperwork.'

'That can wait until Monday. I'll come with you.'

Amelia couldn't help herself and glanced down at his bandaged hand. 'And you're planning to help how exactly?'

'Well, with an attitude like that, perhaps I *won't* offer my help.' His voice was still smooth, still deep, still washed over her like silk, but this time there was a hint of teasing in his tone. 'Instead, I might simply watch you. See if you're as good as Tina says you are, Dr Watson.'

'Terrific.' The word was dry and she turned on her heel, heading towards treatment room one. She wanted to get some distance between them, not have him tag along for an impromptu testing session. Harrison's sexy chuckle encompassed her and she realised he was following her. Why couldn't he just leave her alone? She wasn't in the mood for a test—not when she'd been stuck in this place for goodness knew how many hours. She sighed, trying to pull some energy from somewhere.

'Long shift?'

'And getting longer.'

'Some people would say being snippy isn't the best way to make an impression on your new boss.'

'And some other people would say testing your new employees when they've been working for hours on end isn't going to endear you to them, especially the one who took care of your daughter and returned her safely to your waiting arms.' She faked a smile and he laughed once more.

'You smile so sweetly yet your words are so full of…meaning.' The twinkle in his eyes captivated her for a moment and she wondered just how many other women felt the same way when they looked at him. All she'd heard about him was that he was a widower, his wife having died a few years ago, and apart from that, all Tina had said about their boss had been that he was fair and just. 'Let's get set up,' Harrison said.

'I'm not being snippy,' she said as she started setting things up. 'I'm punchy. There's a difference.'

'Divided by a thin line, Amelia-Jane.'

'It's just Amelia. No one calls me that.'

'Why not? I think it kind of suits you, Amelia-Jane.'

'Bit of a mouthful, though.'

'Well…' Harrison leaned against the cupboards and gave her another quick perusal. 'When we're nice and relaxed like this, I'll call you Amelia-Jane, and when we're busy, I think I'll just bark *"Watson"* and then you'll come running.'

Amelia couldn't help herself this time and laughed, shaking her head and not wanting to be impressed by him. He didn't seem to mind her exhausted attitude, which meant he'd worked long hard shifts and understood how things were near the end.

Wow. Harrison was glad he was leaning against something as the power of her true smile almost made him slide to the ground. How could he not have seen that instant beauty? When she smiled at him like that, he felt it, and that was odd in itself because there was absolutely no room in his life for anything except his job and his daughter. Yet somehow Amelia-Jane Watson, the new English rose with the alluring accent, was intriguing him more with each passing second.

'I can't believe we're discussing my name like this.' She crossed to the sink and washed her hands again, the wail of the ambulance sirens getting closer by the second. 'It's just a name. Right, Harry?'

His smile was slow. 'Make it Harrison, if you value your job and your life, Dr Watson.'

'Don't like it, eh?'

'Not particularly.'

'It doesn't suit you. Harrison does.'

'Thank you and I tend to think that Amelia-Jane suits you better. It's more…English,' he said, and she found herself captivated by him once more.

'You seem very laid back for a director.' Her words were soft and she was astonished to hear them come out sounding intimate.

'That's just the way I am,' he replied. He looked into her eyes and was taken aback at the way his gut twisted with desire. He'd never been so instantly attracted to someone before and he should heed the warning signs. Yet there was something about her…the soothing sound of her voice or the subtle scent of her perfume, or perhaps just the way she didn't seem to be intimidated by her new boss. Oh, yes, she was interesting.

The sirens were loud now, the ambulance obviously pulling into the bay outside before the loud noise ceased. Amelia pulled on a protective gown over her clothes as the doors to A and E slid open a moment later, the paramedics wheeling in the patients.

When she'd finished tying the tapes of her gown, she turned to see Harrison standing at the sink, washing both his hands, his tatty bandage nowhere in sight.

'What do you think you're doing? You'll damage your—' She looked at his hands as she spoke and was surprised to find nothing wrong with either of them. Nothing at all. 'Miraculous recovery?'

'Either that or I'm a very fast healer.'

'You were never hurt, right?'

'My dear Watson, you catch on fast.'

Amelia rolled her eyes and groaned at his pun. 'Thanks, Sherlock. So why *was* your hand bandaged?' The patients were transferred to the A and E beds but she wanted to know.

'Because I hurt my hand—nothing serious—and my daughter insisted on playing doctor and bandaging it for me.'

The cutest little nurse... Realisation dawned on Amelia and she now understood what Yolanda had told her. 'She *fixed* it.' Well, at least that explained the bad bandaging job.

He smiled. 'Yolanda's a very insistent three-year-old.'

'She seems as though she has a strong will. Good luck with that.'

Harrison nodded and rolled his eyes. 'I think I'm

going to need it.' He dried his hands and pulled on a gown to protect his old painting clothes and looked at Amelia for direction.

'What have we got?' she asked the paramedics.

'Two teenagers, both sixteen years of age. Meg and Tad. Found passed out in a classroom by the school cleaner, three six-hundred-mil bottles of vodka next to them.'

'Quite a party.' Amelia pulled on gloves. 'Harrison, take the boy,' she instructed. After all, if he was testing her, surely that meant she was the one in charge. 'Meg? Meg? Can you hear me? I'm Dr Watson. Meg?' She tapped the girl lightly on the cheek and received a slurred response.

'Pupils are enlarged,' the nurse reported. 'BP's down.'

'Why do they do this?' Harrison said as he called again to Tad and received a response. A moment later Tad started to turn green. 'Bucket!' Harrison called and stepped out of the way just in time as Tad spontaneously performed his own gastric lavage.

'Meg's airway is clear,' Amelia reported. 'Let's get the lavage started.' She administered a spray of topical anaesthetic into Meg's mouth before inserting an endo-tracheal tube that would prevent Meg from breathing in the stomach fluids into her lungs.

'Tip her onto her left side,' Amelia directed, and then they lowered her head. Next, she inserted the lubricated stomach tube through Meg's mouth, which went down into the oesophagus and into the stomach. 'Start suction.' She glanced across at Harrison. 'How's Tad?'

'Doing a good job of rejecting what he's swallowed all on his own.'

'Good. Give him activated charcoal with sorbitol-hyperosmotic. That should help speed up the emptying of his intestines. Are their parents here yet?' she asked one of the nurses.

'I believe so.'

'OK. I'll talk to them once we're done.' She looked at Meg and sighed, wondering why the teenager thought binge drinking was good fun. 'Welcome to the party,' she said sadly, then looked across at Tad, who didn't look as though he was having a good time at all. She glanced at Harrison, who seemed to have the same expression on his face as she did.

'Are we having fun yet?' He grimaced as he said the words and shook his head.

When both were stable, she went to talk to the parents, who were embarrassed and concerned as well as furious with their kids. 'Both Tad and Meg will need to stay at least overnight to be monitored. We'd also like them to see one of the social workers here so they can talk about why they did it.'

'There's nothing wrong with my daughter,' Meg's father blustered, and jabbed his finger at Tad's dad. 'It's his fault. It's *his* son who's corrupted my sweet little girl.'

Amelia dealt with the parents and managed to calm them down, conscious of the fact that Harrison was there, watching and listening but not interrupting. When the patients were stable and ready for transfer to a ward, Amelia sat down to write up the case notes, Harrison pulling up a chair beside her and doing the same.

'How did I do, Dr Stapleton? Pass your test?'

Harrison nodded slowly. 'Actually, you weren't too bad.'

'Too bad.' She thought over those words. 'See, if I knew you better, I'd know whether that was praise or not.'

Harrison kept writing the notes, not looking at her. 'It's praise.'

'Oh, goody.' Even though she spoke the words with a hint of sarcasm she was kind of pleased he hadn't found fault. 'If you're finished with the notes, I'll take them around to the ward.'

'Trying to get rid of me, Amelia-Jane?'

She shrugged, conscious of the way his thigh was very close to hers beneath the desk. Once more she could feel the warmth emanating from his body and didn't like the way it was affecting her. He was her boss and nothing more, but right now she wouldn't mind a bit of space to get her mind in gear and to try and figure out just what it was about him that seemed to knock her off balance. 'I simply thought you might like to get home and spend what's left of your Friday with your daughter.'

'What if I haven't finished testing you?'

'Well, unless you're going to test me on how fast I can clock off and leave the hospital, you're going to have to wait until another day for further testing because I am going home.' With that, she gathered up the two sets of case notes. 'See you on Monday, Dr Stapleton.'

'If not before, Dr Watson.'

Amelia tried not to smile as she walked to the ward. He was nice. He was good-looking. He was even funny. At the moment she couldn't find anything not to like about him and that was bad. She didn't want to like her new boss, or at least she didn't want to feel anything other than enjoying a platonic working relationship with him. Somehow, though, during the short acquaintance they'd had, Harrison Stapleton had made a lasting impression.

She returned to the change rooms and after having a quick shower she re-dressed, slipping her feet into her shoes and brushing her hair. At least now she felt more human and could return to her seaside holiday apartment to relax in peace and quiet for the remainder of the night. Thankfully, she'd found a place within two blocks from the hospital and therefore had no need for a car. The times when she worked late, she took a taxi home. Besides, the area in which she'd chosen to live was across the road from the beach and a street away from a shopping centre. The perfect place to complete her final months of training.

Amelia picked up her bag, paged Tina to let her know she was leaving the hospital and headed for the door. As she stepped outside into the mid-March evening, glad the sun was still up, thanks to daylight saving, she was startled to find Harrison Stapleton standing there, leaning against the wall. He quickly stood upright when he saw her.

'Ah, Amelia-Jane. There you are. I thought I might have missed you.'

'Something wrong?'

'No. No.' He shifted and shoved his hands into his pockets. 'I, er…just wanted to thank you again for looking after Yolanda. She's everything to me and I went crazy with worry when Mrs D. told me she was missing. So…er, thanks.'

'It's fine. Everything worked out.' She hunted in her handbag for her sunglasses, still getting used to the fact that March meant the end of summer rather than the end of winter, as she'd been used to all her life. She found the glasses but didn't put them on, looking at Harrison. 'Was there something else?'

'Do you have a car?' he asked.

'No. I don't live far from here.'

'Neither do I. Which street?'

'The Esplanade.'

'Really? What number?'

Amelia thought for a moment. 'Uh…number 375. I'm staying in one of the holiday apartment complexes.'

Harrison shook his head. 'That's two doors down from where I live. I'll walk you home.'

Amelia was startled. 'That's OK. I'm fine.'

His grin was immediate. 'We're both walking the same way, Amelia-Jane. It would be ridiculous to walk down the street and ignore each other.' He had no idea why he was insisting she agree, apart from the fact that he wanted to get to know her a bit more. While he told himself it was all strictly business as he hadn't yet received her file from her previous hospital and she could perhaps fill him in on some details, Harrison knew it went a little deeper than that.

The two of them had some sort of strange connection. He couldn't explain it. They'd certainly got along well, both while they'd been enjoying silly banter and whilst they'd been working.

He watched her now, seeing her indecision, and for some reason he felt like giving her a testimony to let her know that he was safe, that he was a good guy, that he would never harm her. She glanced at him and he smiled, and when she slowly returned that smile he was stunned by the instant hit to his solar plexus. In that moment, Harrison realised he *liked* Amelia-Jane Watson. *Really* liked her. As a man liked a woman…a woman he could become interested in.

That had *never* happened to him before.

CHAPTER TWO

'I GUESS it does seem silly,' Amelia said, bringing Harrison back from his musings.

'Huh? Oh, right.' He indicated the main gate to the hospital. 'Shall we go, then?'

'Of course.' Amelia slipped on her sunglasses as they headed out, conscious of keeping a bit of distance between them so they didn't accidentally bump hands as they walked. Both were silent and she felt the weight of it. She searched for a suitable topic and came up with the first polite level of small-talk she could think of. 'The weather here is certainly nicer than back where I live.'

Harrison nodded. 'Tina said you're from the Lake District.'

'That's right. My parents have lived in Barrow all my life.'

'It's a nice area.'

'You've been there?'

'On my honeymoon, actually. We…ah…toured that area. I'm a widower,' he added quickly, in case she though he was married.

'I'd heard.' Amelia couldn't believe how uncomfortable she felt. She'd liked what she'd seen so far where her new boss was concerned and while she had no intention of getting involved with him, it seemed a little strange to be walking down the street, discussing his late wife.

'Did you like it?'

'I did. Inga wasn't all that taken with it. London was more her scene.'

'Oh,' Amelia said again, wishing she could think of something else to say. 'London's not really my thing.'

'Too noisy?'

'Yes.'

'Me, too.'

A group of teenagers riding bikes came up onto the footpath near them before whizzing past, causing Harrison to step aside and inadvertently bump into Amelia. His hands came up to her arms to steady her so they didn't fall, his chest pressed against hers.

'Sorry.' He quickly regained his balance, trying desperately not to concentrate on the way Amelia felt in his arms. She was his colleague, a very beautiful and desirable colleague who would be leaving his world in just three short months and it wouldn't do him any good to go forgetting that. Dragging in a sobering breath, he finally found the will, the strength to set her from him, putting distance between their bodies, but found he was still unable to completely let go. It was an unspoken personal rule to avoid relationships with hospital personnel, especially if they were members of his department, but something about Amelia seemed to be reeling him in, making him forget everything except the way he felt right now.

'Are you all right?' Harrison's tone was deep and the sound resonated through her body, not helping Amelia to control her reaction to him. His hands were still on her arms, warm and firm yet not hurting her at all. A moment ago, when she'd been cradled in his arms, arms that were strong and protective, she'd felt a sense of perfection wash over her. She couldn't help the reaction she experienced at his touch and it was as though her body was reacting completely on its own, without consulting her brain.

'Good,' he said when she nodded that she was OK. 'Kids never look where they're going.' Reluctantly, he eased his hands open, his fingers trailing softly down her arms until they dropped heavily back to his sides.

The warmth, the tingles his touch had created stayed with her even after he'd removed his hands and for a moment Amelia found it impossible to get her legs to work. Instead, she simply stood there, looking up at him, trying to control her fingers, which itched to brush his hair back from his forehead where a dark brown lock had fallen. It was then she realised she was trembling and she clasped her hands together to try and control it.

'Are you sure you're all right?' Harrison asked, looking more closely at her, and Amelia looked away.

'I'm fine. Really.' The moment had gone, passed, and now she could hopefully begin to function like a human being again. She shifted her bag further onto her shoulder and nodded again for emphasis.

'Only one more block to go. Think we can accomplish it undamaged?' Harrison asked, with a small smile.

Was he talking about the reckless kids or what had just transpired between the two of them? Amelia decided to interpret it as the former because the latter simply threatened to break the control she'd just managed to obtain over her senses. 'It could be risky,' she countered, and was pleased when he laughed, the sound washing over her like a warm, comfortable blanket. 'I think we should chance it.'

'Excellent.' They started walking once again, both of them keeping a little more distance between them. Amelia glanced in the shop windows they were walking by and saw one laden with Easter chocolates.

Harrison groaned when he saw them.

'You don't like Easter?' she asked.

'I don't like the constant badgering for chocolates,' he said.

'Yolanda?'

He nodded. 'It's astounding. Females seemed to be genetically attracted to chocolate and Yolanda is no exception. She's even gone so far as to get the latest Easter catalogue, sit down with me and point out everything she wants.'

Amelia couldn't help but smile. 'Definitely a girl who knows what she wants.'

'That's my baby.' Harrison's smile was that of a doting dad. 'How about you?'

She smiled. 'Do you mean have I sat down with my father and gone through the Easter sale catalogues with him?'

'Exactly.' He was pleased they seemed to share the same warped sense of humour. 'Actually, I meant are you a girl who knows what she wants?'

Amelia thought about it for a moment. 'Um…most of the time, I guess. I don't always get it, of course, but as far as Easter chocolate goes, well, that one's easy.'

'It is?'

'Yes. I'm not a big chocolate fan.'

'Really?' His eyebrows hit his hairline. 'You don't like chocolate?'

Amelia shrugged. 'I'd rather have something savoury than sweet.'

'Interesting.' Harrison looked very thoughtful.

'What? Never met a woman who didn't go for chocolates? I don't like fresh flowers either.'

'Now you're starting to scare me. Just when I think I have the fairer sex worked out.'

Amelia found it hard to repress her smile. Harrison was revealing himself as a very sweet man with a playful charm that was difficult not to respond to. She wished for strength as she would need to keep herself under tight control.

Given the direction in which they were walking, they came across Harrison's house first and as they stopped outside she looked up, admiring the beautiful two-storey beach house. Its double-glazed glass front would let in a lot of the sun but keep a lot of the heat out, as well as providing wonderful views of the ocean.

'Nice place,' she said.

Harrison shrugged nonchalantly. 'It's nothing special but it's home.'

Amelia laughed and he pointed to the apartment two doors down. 'Do you like where you're staying?'

'Yes, I do. The apartment is clean, comfortable, came fully furnished and was a reasonable price. Also, there are your beaches.' She sighed as she looked across the road to where the glistening golden sand and the dark blue water shone. 'Australia has the most beautiful beaches, in my opinion.'

'You'll get no argument from me. I guess the sand here is a little more...um...golden than Brighton?'

Amelia nodded. 'It's also *sand*, which is very nice to walk on.'

Harrison agreed. 'You know, we have our own Brighton beach.' He pointed south. 'Further up that way, and I guarantee the sand is just as nice as here.'

'I'll have to check it out.'

Before either of them could say another word, a high-pitched squeal pierced the air and both turned to see Yolanda running down the front path, arms open as she hurtled herself towards Harrison.

Instantly, he bent down and scooped her up when she got close enough, her arms closing about his neck with glee. 'Daddy. Daddy.'

Harrison hugged her close and glanced over at the doorway where a woman stood. 'Hi, Mrs D.,' he called, and waved one hand.

'You're back earlier than we thought,' the woman said, her strong English accent resonating through the air. 'We've just woken from our rest and have finished making some biscuits.'

'Dey are berry yummy, Daddy,' Yolanda assured him.

Amelia took in the scene and took a step away. 'I'd better get going,' she said. 'See you at work.'

'Uh…' Harrison shifted Yolanda to his hip, his arms still firm around her as the little girl planted a few kisses on his cheek. 'Would you like to come in?'

'It's fine. I don't want to intrude.'

'Oh, nonsense.' Mrs D. beckoned them inside. 'It's the least we can do for you helping us out with Yolanda earlier. I'll go put the kettle on and we can all sit down and have a nice cup of tea.'

'Half an hour,' Harrison said, and started up the garden path.

'Are you sure?' Amelia hesitated, not sure if she should accept, although tea and biscuits with Harrison and his family sounded very nice.

'Come on. Mrs D.'s right. Look upon it as our way of saying thank you for finding Yolanda.' Harrison angled his head towards his home and Amelia decided it couldn't hurt. As she walked in, she admired the décor and wondered whether he'd hired a decorator, but as she continued through the house to the rear, where the kitchen was situated, she passed a room that was bare except for drop sheets, ladder and paint tins.

'Doing a bit of renovating?'

Harrison smiled and looked down at his clothes. 'It relaxes me.'

'Harrison's almost done the whole house,' Mrs D. said as Amelia walked around the kitchen bench. 'Please, dear, have a seat,' she said, pointing to the stools. 'I'm Mrs Deveraux or Mrs D., as Harrison so eloquently calls me.'

'Forgive me my manners,' Harrison said as he deposited Yolanda on a stool. 'Mrs D., this is Amelia-Jane, a new registrar all the way from your homeland.'

'Stop teasing her, Harrison,' Mrs D. admonished. 'How do you take your tea, dear?'

'Black, thank you.'

Harrison continued. 'Mrs D. was a dear friend of my mother's and sleeps in the back bedroom where she keeps telling me she's quite comfortable and doesn't want me rearranging furniture or repainting her walls.'

'Quite right,' Mrs D. said as she pulled bone china mugs from the cupboard.

'And you remember Yolanda,' Harrison continued, dropping a kiss on his daughter's head.

'How could I forget?'

'Do you remember Amelia-Jane from the hospital?' Harrison asked his daughter.

'Meel-ya,' Yolanda said, but didn't bother making eye contact until she had a biscuit secured in each hand.

'It's good to see you again.' Amelia smiled at the gorgeous little girl, determined to ignore the emptiness inside she always felt on meeting well-loved children. It had been clear within the first few seconds of seeing Harrison with his daughter that Yolanda was very special to him and she was pleased to find he was a man who appreciated the important things in life.

She pasted a smile on her face and pushed aside the thoughts that she would never have such a beautiful child of her own. It was something she was still trying to accept and whenever she was faced with such a touching scene, it made it all the harder.

The tea was lovely and the biscuits were mouthwatering. When Amelia said as much, Yolanda took full responsibility.

'*I* did it. *I* mixed da flour. *I* mixed da…da…'

'Sugar,' Mrs D. supplied.

'Shoogar,' Yolanda repeated, and climbed down from the stool. 'Come see dolly.'

Amelia blinked at the quick change in topic but allowed herself to be tugged away by the three-year-old, glancing at Harrison who lifted an eyebrow but didn't say a word. Instead, he followed as Yolanda pulled Amelia into her bedroom, which was painted in pink and white with a border of flowers around the edge near the ceiling. A pink and white bed was against the wall opposite the wardrobe and a pink and white bookshelf was against the other wall. Soft toys were all around, and a doctor's set, complete with bandages, lay on the bed, but in pride of place in the middle of the room sat a beautiful dolls' house.

'Ta-da!' She dropped Amelia's hand and ran over to the dolls' house. 'My daddy made it.' There was pride in her voice and Amelia looked at Harrison, who was leaning against the doorjamb. He merely shrugged as though it was nothing.

'My daddy made da shelves.' Yolanda ran to the bookshelves. 'And he made da bed.' She ran to the bed. 'And da *dollies'* house.' She said the word as though it were a sweet she couldn't get enough of, her eyes wide as she lay down next to the dolls' house and opened the front panel.

'Quite the carpenter.' Amelia glanced at Harrison, who allowed himself a little smile. She sat down on the floor, being careful of her skirt, and looked inside.

'Is pink and white,' Yolanda said proudly.

'Do you like pink and white?' Amelia asked, already knowing the answer, and Yolanda nodded enthusiastically.

'However did you guess?' Harrison walked over and sat down next to Yolanda. 'I'm sure when she eventually changes her mind, I'll have to repaint everything all over again.'

'Perhaps she won't change.' Harrison looked doubtful but Amelia nodded. 'My favourite colour is red and has been ever since I can remember. I certainly haven't changed, nor am I about to.'

'Favourite colour is red, doesn't like chocolates or flowers, prefers savoury to sweet and has black tea, no milk, no sugar.' He ticked the points off on his fingers. Amelia was also the only member of his staff he'd seen Yolanda bond with. His daughter was very picky and the fact she'd gone to Amelia with no hesitation whatsoever spoke volumes about the English doctor's character.

'Making a list?' she asked, wondering whether she should be scared or flattered.

'And checking it twice.' He raised his eyebrows. 'Gotta find out who's naughty and who's nice.'

Amelia laughed. 'It's almost Easter, Harrison. Not Christmas.'

'I like to be prepared.'

'Easter!' Yolanda squealed loudly and he immediately hushed her.

'Little softer, please, pumpkin.'

'Easter. Easter. Chocolate. Chocolate.' Yolanda stood up and jumped around the room, clapping her hands.

'See what I mean? Obsessed with Easter.'

Amelia watched the little girl, noting that she still wore a nappy and also that her speech wasn't as advanced as it could be for a three-year-old. Then again, all children developed at different rates but she wondered if Harrison had picked up on anything.

'Come and play with your dolls,' Harrison said, and in the next instant Yolanda was back on the floor, lying on her stomach, picking up a doll and handing it to her father.

'Dis one for you, Daddy, toz you da boy.'

Amelia smiled as Harrison took the male doll and straightened his clothes.

'Dis one for you, toz you a gel.' Amelia found a doll with long blonde hair thrust into her hands.

'Oh. Thank you.'

Harrison's gleam was one of satisfaction. 'Didn't think you were going to get away that easily, did you?' He cleared his throat and walked his doll over to Yolanda's. 'Hello, there, my little girl. Are you ready for the party? My, my, that is a pretty dress you're wearing.'

Yolanda answered him with her doll while Amelia simply sat there and watched the two of them. It was such a precious moment, one of the ones that if she had her choice of capturing and freezing it, she would immediately accept.

'Is dere chocolate at da party?' Yolanda's doll asked.

'Most certainly. Lots and lots of chocolate,' Harrison answered, and Yolanda's doll jumped up and down just as the little girl herself had been doing a few minutes ago.

Amelia's heart welled up with need and longing and to her disgust she felt tears begin to blur her vision. Biting her lip, she tried to control them and took a few deep breaths. It simply wasn't fair that she would never have this when she longed for it with every fibre of her being.

When Harrison glanced at her, his face instantly changed. 'What's wrong?' he asked in his normal voice.

Amelia shook her head and forced a smile. 'Nothing.' She handed the doll back to Yolanda. 'She's a very pretty doll, Yolanda. I'm pleased to see you take such good care of her.'

'Berry prwetty dolly,' Yolanda agreed, and took the doll from her.

'I have to go,' Amelia said and carefully levered herself up from the floor.

'Now?' Harrison said.

'I have a few things to do, plus I've just finished a very long shift.' She looked down at Yolanda. 'Goodbye, Yolanda. I'll see you another time.'

'Bye,' the little girl called, more interested in her dolls than in anything else.

Harrison scrambled to his feet. 'Daddy will be back in a minute, pumpkin.'

'O'tay.'

They walked to the kitchen and Amelia picked up her bag and thanked Mrs D. for the tea. 'It was lovely. Thank you.'

'You're most welcome, dear. Drop by again soon.'

Amelia wasn't sure whether that was going to be possible or not, so she merely smiled before heading through to the front of the house, aware of Harrison following behind her. She had no idea what was currently happening between herself and Harrison, or whether or not it would go anywhere.

At the front door she turned to face him. 'Thanks. It was nice of you to invite me.'

'I'll walk you to your door,' he said.

'It's all right. It's not necessary,' she started, but he'd closed the front door behind him and stepped past her, heading down the path.

'It's no trouble.'

Amelia shook her head, realising it was pointless to try and argue with him.

'So…are you sure you're all right?' he asked as they walked past the house between his home and her apartment complex.

Amelia rubbed a hand against her temple and sighed. She didn't want to talk about it. Not now and not with him, but how did she say that without intriguing him further or possibly hurting his feelings?

'It's nothing. I… She's just so gorgeous. Besides, there are things I need to do.'

Harrison nodded slowly. 'Mind if I don't believe you?'

'That I have things to do? Why would I lie about that?'

'There's something you're not telling me.'

'There's a lot I'm not telling you. Harrison, we only

met a few hours ago.' She stopped at the corner of the apartment complex. 'I don't find it easy to open up to people. It's just who I am.'

'So there is something bothering you?'

'A lot of things bother me, just as I'm sure the same could be said for you or Mrs D. or anyone else for that matter. It doesn't mean I want to talk about them all.'

Harrison shrugged, realising he'd have to let it go if he didn't want to upset her. That wasn't his intention but neither could he help the concern that had gripped him at seeing her eyes mist up the way they had. He knew it was far better for him to maintain a professional distance between the two of them. 'Fair enough.' He pointed to the building. 'Home at last, eh? Go and rest, Dr Watson. I'll see you at work.'

The next week seemed to fly by and Amelia didn't see much of Harrison as they were on different shifts. But on Thursday, when she was on a regular day shift, he sought her out in the cafeteria.

'Is this seat taken?' Harrison asked, and she looked up from the book she'd been reading, trying to squash the feeling of pleasure at seeing him.

'Hi. Uh...no. Please, sit.' She closed her book.

'Is the book good?' he asked, and she shrugged.

'I've read it before. So, how are things?'

'Good. I heard you had afternoon tea with my daughter yesterday.'

Amelia nodded slowly, concerned at what his reaction would be to the news. 'I did. I met Mrs D. and Yolanda on the beach when I was taking a walk and they invited me back. I hope you don't mind.'

'No. Yolanda was happy to have someone to play

dolls with. At least, she told me your dolls had gone to a party with lots of chocolate.'

Amelia smiled. 'They did.'

'That's good.' He nodded and unwrapped his sandwich. 'So, tell me, Amelia-Jane, what have you been doing the past few days, besides working, walking along the beach and having afternoon teas?'

'Hmm. Let me think. I've been working, walking along the beach and having afternoon teas.'

'Just as I thought,' he said, and she laughed. He enjoyed the sound of her laughter and liked the way her face lit up, her blue eyes sparkling with merriment. He took a bite of his sandwich and they talked about the patients they'd seen and other general hospital matters. It was amazing how much they agreed on and Harrison was pleased with the way Amelia seemed to be settling in with the rest of the staff.

'That's good to hear,' he said. 'Staffing issues can be real nightmares, especially when employing doctors from overseas. You never know exactly what you're going to get until they arrive.'

Amelia raised her eyebrows. 'Very flattering, I'm sure.'

'Oh, not you, of course.' Harrison looked contrite, as though he'd temporarily forgotten she was from overseas, or perhaps he'd said it on purpose just to tease her.

'Why not?' she prompted.

'Because you came highly recommended.'

She smiled. 'Tina's a good friend.'

'You've known each other long?'

'Quite some time.' Her pager beeped and she sighed and slowly rose to her feet. 'Sorry I can't keep you company while you finish your lunch.'

Harrison shrugged. 'You're better off going. If you

make Rosie wait, you won't get a moment's worth of peace.'

'Who's in charge of this department?'

'Uh…me?'

'Or so you think,' she agreed. 'See you later, Harrison.' As she walked away from the cafeteria she was surprised at how happy she felt. He really was a nice man and she found she liked talking to him.

She bumped into Tina on her way to A and E. Her friend had a large smile on her face. 'I saw you talking to Harrison,' she said in a sing-song voice.

'Yeah. He just came and sat down to eat his lunch.' Amelia put her paperback into the pocket of her white coat.

'Had any more afternoon teas?' Tina raised her pinky in the air and mimicked Amelia's accent.

'Ah, yesterday, actually, but only with his daughter and housekeeper.'

'Oh. How disappointing.'

'Not really.' Amelia dropped her voice as she said, 'You know how difficult it is for me to open up to other people. It takes me a while to feel comfortable around strangers.'

'And you really get the opportunity to do that when you're moving hospitals every three months.' Tina's sarcasm was evident. 'Why on earth did you choose to do your twelve-month overseas rotation in four different hospitals?'

'I wanted to see as much of Australia as I could. You know that.'

'I also know that's not the real reason. Anyway, I have to say that you look very comfortable around Harrison.'

Amelia sighed and nodded sadly. 'And that's a problem.'

'Why? He's single, he's good-looking, he's funny.'

'He has a daughter.'

'That should be a bonus as far as you're concerned. He won't be too bothered about you not being able to have children because he's already got one.'

Amelia stopped and looked at her friend, more than used to her bluntness. 'I can't get involved. I leave at the end of June and I have plans back in England.'

'Plans such as not staying and working in one hospital for any extended length of time?'

Amelia started walking again, faster this time, her annoyance showing. 'Plans such as experiencing a variety of situations around the world,' Amelia countered. 'There's nothing wrong with travelling while I have the opportunity, Tina.'

'Travelling? No. Running away? Yes.'

They took the stairs to A and E. 'I am not running away.'

'No. It's impossible to run away from yourself.'

Amelia huffed. 'Go home and sleep,' she told Tina. 'I need to work.'

'All right. Hey, I noticed you're rostered off on Saturday. Do you want to meet for coffee? I don't start work until eleven.'

'Sure.'

'We can talk more about you know who.'

'Goodbye, Tina.' Amelia waved and headed for the nurses' station.

The two registrars met for coffee on Saturday morning and managed to squeeze in a bit of shopping before Tina started work. Amelia bought a new pair of shoes, two new skirts for work, three new tops and a new jacket.

'Planning to go out on a few dates?' Tina teased.

'No. The clothes are cheaper here than back home. That's all.'

'Oh, good excuse.'

'It's the truth.'

'Look, why don't you admit that you like Harrison Stapleton?'

'Why?'

'Because at least then you can do something about it.'

'Or not.'

'He's a great guy. Everyone at work likes and respects him and personally I think it would be wonderful if you two started dating. You're perfect for each other.'

Amelia opened her mouth to refute Tina's claims but decided it wasn't worth the effort. Tina had a bee in her bonnet and that was fine. Just so long as it didn't come buzzing around her.

'See? You can't even deny it.'

She sighed. 'Fine. I like him. All right? Are you happy now?'

'You should go for it.'

'Tina. I've already told you I don't have ti—'

'Save it, sister. I've heard it all before.' Tina checked her watch and then shrieked. 'Oops. Gotta go. I'll see you when I see you.'

Amelia rolled her eyes and waved then decided to go and have another quick cup of coffee before she went looking for a new pair of earrings. She was sitting down to enjoy it when she looked up and was surprised to see Harrison. He was coming out of the shop opposite and had Yolanda on his shoulders, her brown eyes shining with delight. His hands were on her legs, holding her steady, but she sat straight without a care in the world and obviously queen of all she surveyed. Amelia couldn't help smiling at the picture they made.

Mrs Deveraux came out of the shop behind him, carrying a shopping bag. Harrison asked her something and she looked around, then pointed to the coffee-shop where Amelia was. Harrison spotted her straight away and waved, heading in her direction.

'Amelia-Jane,' he said as they walked over. 'Fancy meeting you here.'

'Fancy,' she replied, and said hello to Mrs D. and Yolanda. Everyone seemed to stand still for a moment, no one wanting to make a move to stay or go, and in the end Amelia realised it would be up to her to make the first move. She cleared her throat and indicated the empty chairs at her table. 'Would you care to join me?'

'Excellent idea.' Harrison instantly pulled out two chairs and lifted Yolanda from his shoulders. 'Time for a drink, wouldn't you say?' he asked his daughter as he planted a kiss on her cheek and sat with her on his knee. 'Mrs D. could certainly use the break.'

'Definitely,' Mrs Deveraux replied, putting the shopping bags on the floor. 'Time for tea.'

Harrison glanced briefly at the menu then gave their order to the waitress who came to attend them. 'AJ? You right for a drink?'

She opened her mouth to say something but stopped at the abbreviation of her name. It was what her family called her and although she had no objection to the name, it surprised her that someone she didn't really know that well was using a nickname so soon in their acquaintance. It made them seem more familiar, closer, intimate somehow, and that was hardly the case.

'I'm fine, thank you.'

When the waitress had gone, Harrison leaned on the table. 'Is it all right if I call you that?'

'Uh…sure. You just surprised me. It's more a family pet name. Just sounds strange hearing it in this environment but, hey, it's just a name.'

He shrugged. 'AJ suits you.'

'What? Two letters. Short, sharp and shiny?'

Harrison chuckled at that. 'No.' For a moment she thought he was going to say more but he didn't.

'Teaset. Teaset,' Yolanda said, and climbed down from his knee to rummage around in a big bag Mrs D. had been carrying.

'Yes, here you go, dear,' the woman said, and pulled out a container, opening it for Yolanda. The girl climbed back onto her father's lap and withdrew little plastic cups and saucers and a teapot then proceeded to pour them all 'tea'. Mrs Deveraux's phone rang and she answered it with a sigh, looking at the name on the display.

'Excuse me,' she said, and stood again, leaving them alone while she took her call.

Harrison looked from Yolanda to Amelia and back again. 'Yolanda. Do you remember Amelia-Jane? She came and played dolls with you.'

Yolanda nodded her head, curls bobbing all over the place.

'Can you say hello to Amelia?'

'Hey-yo, Meel-ya,' she said, and again Amelia had the feeling something wasn't quite right with the little girl. Then Yolanda handed Amelia a cup and saucer, and she willingly sipped the imaginary tea, enjoying the child's delight. 'Tareful. Is hot,' Yolanda warned.

'Quite right,' Amelia said, and blew on it first. She glanced at Harrison, who seemed to be watching her closely, and she began to feel as though she was under a microscope. She handed the cup back to Yolanda. 'Thank you for the tea. It was delicious.'

'She just loves tea parties,' Harrison said, still watching Amelia closely.

'What little girl doesn't?'

'Did you?'

'Most certainly. I used to do exactly what she's doing and force everyone to drink their imaginary tea. That was until I graduated to sugar water.' She shook her head. 'I can't say my parents were too fond of that.'

'You're an only child?'

'Yes.' That was all she was going to say on the subject.

Harrison sipped his imaginary tea and realised Amelia wasn't going to say anything else about her family—at least, not this time. 'When I saw this teaset I couldn't resist it, and I'm glad I bought it. She only plays with this one when we're out and about and has a pink one at home for her dolls.'

Amelia smiled at the 'pink' part. 'Naturally. It wouldn't do to just have *one* teaset. How ordinary!' Harrison laughed, enjoying the way she drawled her vowels. 'So, how's the E-a-s-t-e-r shopping going?' She deliberately spelt out the word so she didn't set Yolanda off again, jumping about the shop.

Harrison returned her smile and nodded. 'Almost finished. Hard to believe it's just next weekend.'

Yolanda poured the tea again and both adults dutifully drank from their tiny cups before returning them.

'So…how's your week been?' Harrison asked.

'Busy,' she said. 'Although I'm sure you know that.'

'I've read the stats and reports.' He paused. 'And you've settled into your apartment all right? Nothing you need?'

'No. Everything's just fine.'

'Your paperwork still hasn't arrived,' he said. 'Brisbane General are slack in the admin department. If it wasn't for Tina vouching for you, I'd be calling the police to do a background check.'

'Really?'

'No.' He laughed, enjoying her gullibility.

Amelia watched as his eyes filled with merriment at her expense, not that she minded. Still, it didn't seem fair that his eyes should be so mesmerising, so deep, so rich and vibrant in colour that it would be all too easy just to sit there and look at him all day long. 'I need to go.' She started to gather up her packages at the same time Mrs D. returned to the table and the waitress brought their drinks.

'Stay.' The one word came from Harrison's lips before she'd even managed to push herself to her feet. She looked at him and wondered why it was so important to him that she be there.

Harrison couldn't believe that he wanted to spend more time with her. He was already behind in his renovation schedule due to thinking about her too much. The way she smiled, the way she laughed at his silly jokes and the way they seemed to be on the same wavelength.

'Please, stay. We'd feel terrible if we thought we'd driven you off.'

'You're not driving me off. I have more shopping to do.'

'Shopping!' Yolanda said loudly, froth all over her lips from the warmed milk she was drinking. It was enough to break the ice and they all smiled.

'She *loves* coming to the shops,' he explained.

'And you?'

'Loathe it. Especially on Saturdays when there are more people here.'

Amelia nodded, understanding exactly what he meant about the amount of people. It was one of the reasons she usually preferred to have her days off in the middle of the week. 'Really, though. I need to get going. It was nice to see you all again.'

Why did he look so disappointed? It was strange. Ridiculous, but this time he didn't protest. 'Fair enough.' He stood and for a moment, she wasn't sure why. Then she realised he was just being a gentleman and the action endeared him to her. 'See you at work,' he said with a nod.

When she'd walked out of the coffee-shop she paused and momentarily closed her eyes. Harrison Stapleton was nothing more to her than a boss and colleague. She headed towards the escalators, deciding she'd head home, suddenly feeling exhausted. She was halfway up towards the second floor of the indoor shopping mall when a loud scream pierced the air.

She turned just in time to see a pregnant woman lose her balance on the down escalator and tumble head over heels, knocking into another man who, though he was pushed quite heavily, managed not to lose his balance and somehow stopped the woman in one motion.

Amelia pushed ahead of the people in front, stepping quickly off before making her way down the descending escalator again, pushing her way through the people staring in horror and disbelief at what had just happened. 'Let me through. I'm a doctor,' she called. A little boy was crying as she rushed towards the woman who was now lying on the floor at the base of the escalators.

Amelia stepped off and put her bags down, reaching the woman at the same time another person came into view. She glanced up and almost breathed a sigh of relief.

'Harrison. Thank goodness.'

CHAPTER THREE

HARRISON quickly took in the situation and turned to the big burly man, who was kneeling next to the woman. 'Are you her husband?'

'No. No. She bumped into me.'

'He caught her,' Amelia supplied.

'Right. Press the emergency stop button, then get the rest of these people off and out of the way. Then get hold of the shopping mall security. We'll need an ambulance.'

'Are you a doctor?' the man asked as Harrison crouched down beside the woman and put his hand on her abdomen. Amelia took the woman's pulse and called to her.

'We both are,' Harrison stated, his tone brooking no argument. 'Just do it.'

'Can you hear me?' Amelia called. The woman was groggy and moaning but conscious. There was blood flowing from somewhere and she searched, finding a large gash on the woman's arm. She pressed her hand firmly to the area while feeling the woman's head with her other hand. 'What's your name?' No answer. 'Stay with me,' Amelia urged. 'What's your name?'

'Mummy? Mummy?' The little boy was sitting at the woman's feet, crying.

'What's your name, sport?' Harrison asked, as he continued to check their patient for any fractures. The little boy just continued to cry and Amelia's heart went out to him. 'My name's Harrison and this is AJ. We're both doctors and we're going to help Mummy, OK?'

Amelia lifted the woman's eyelids and was pleased when her pupils reacted to the light emanating from the shops in the centre. Her breathing was shallow and starting to come in gasps. Amelia carefully continued to feel the woman's head, checking for contusions, not surprised when she felt something wet and sticky in the woman's hair.

'She's having contractions,' Harrison said.

'Braxton-Hicks?'

'Feels like it at the moment but a fall like that—'

'Can induce labour,' she finished. 'I can feel two lacerations to the head. Both open wounds—not bad, though. Can you hear me?' she called again, and once more received a moan in response. 'Good.'

'Mummy?' The little boy had obviously had enough of sitting there, still not seeing his mother move. He stood and tried to push past Harrison in order to get closer to his mum. Amelia's heart contracted tighter and the urge to simply pick him up and hold him close was almost overwhelming. People were everywhere, milling around them, walking past and not interested. At least the escalator had been switched off so people weren't coming down in droves.

Harrison shifted so the boy could come closer. 'Here you go, champ. Can you help me by holding Mummy's hand? You talk to her because I'll bet she loves to hear you talk.'

'My mummy?'

'Yes. We're going to help your mummy,' Amelia said. 'You hold her hand. What's your name, sweetheart?'

'Ethan?' It was the woman who mumbled the word.

'Mummy?' Ethan's big blue eyes widened even more. Poor lamb. He couldn't be more than three. 'Mummy. Get up. Get up.' His tears were starting to flow now.

'Ethan's fine,' Harrison immediately assured the woman.

'What's your name?' Amelia asked.

'Liv Davis,' the woman murmured.

'I'm Amelia, this is Harrison. We're doctors.'

'The baby?'

'Is fine but starting to get impatient,' Harrison said gently. 'You have a few other injuries, too, Liv. It looks like you may have fractured your shinbone, given the amount of swelling around it. You have lacerations to your legs, arms and head, but you've been very lucky.'

'Ethan?'

'He's fine. Scared, but fine.'

Liv seemed to relax a little but Amelia saw her squeeze her son's hand in an attempt to reassure him as best she could. It was the bond between mother and child and she felt the familiar sadness touch her heart.

'AJ,' Harrison said and she looked over at him. 'You all right?'

'Fine.' She nodded, quick to assure him. Thankfully the security team from the shopping mall arrived on the scene, bringing a first-aid kit and a stretcher so their attention was taken up with getting Liv organised.

'Excellent,' Harrison said, as Amelia opened the kit and ripped open a pad, pressing it to Liv's skull where she'd previously been applying pressure. With her other hand she found a bandage, pulled the sterile dressing open. She began to wind the bandage around Liv's head, holding the pad in place. Next she applied a padded bandage to Liv's arm, which would probably end up needing sutures, but they had other things to concentrate on for the moment.

'Harrison?'

Amelia looked up and saw Mrs Deveraux standing there, holding Yolanda's hand.

'Ah, Mrs D. Good.' Harrison's voice was calm. 'This is Ethan.' He indicated the boy. 'We're going to move Ethan's mummy to a nice quiet room while we wait for the ambulance. Perhaps you and Yolanda can help look after Ethan.'

'Of course,' replied Mrs D.

'Daddy.' Harrison's daughter came to stand right beside her father, leaning on his back a little. 'Are you doh-ing to made a baby?' she said, pointing to the woman's stomach.

'Deliver,' Harrison automatically corrected his daughter's word usage. 'Possibly. Come and say hello to Ethan.'

'Hey-yo. I'm free.' She held up her fingers to indicate her age, almost shoving them in poor Ethan's face. 'I'm a *big* gel,' she said proudly.

'*I'm* free, too.' Ethan puffed his chest out as he stood and looked at Yolanda. He was still holding his mother's hand but he had something different to interest him—a bossy girl.

Amelia had finished bandaging the head. 'Pain relief? We need to give her something before we move her.'

'Liv? Are you allergic to anything?' Harrison asked.

'Not that I know of?'

'Did you have any problems with Ethan's delivery?'

'He was breech.'

Harrison put his hands on Liv's stomach again and felt the position of the baby. 'Not this one.'

Liv groaned and her muscles tensed and she started to push.

Amelia and Harrison looked at each other before they both burst into action. 'We need to get her moved now.' Harrison called to the security man. 'Have you had first-aid training?'

'Yes.'

'Right. I need something to use as a splint and I need it now. Amelia, get me some bandages out. Bring that stretcher closer. Mrs D., please, try to distract Ethan so he's out of the way while we move his mother. Little ones have a habit of getting underfoot right at the wrong time,' he said by way of explanation.

'Sounds like experience talking,' Amelia said, knowing Liv was aware of everything they were saying. 'You'll be fine, Liv. We just need to sort your leg out before we move you somewhere more private.'

'My back hurts. My stomach. The baby!' Liv's voice broke on the last word and she started to cry. 'This isn't fair. It isn't fair.'

'I know. You're doing great, though. We're here, we're looking after you. You'll be at the hospital before you know it. Unfortunately, at the moment we can't give you any pain medication, not until one of us does an internal examination. You might already be in labour,' Amelia said as she opened the packet of tissues from the first-aid box and dabbed at Liv's eyes.

'Ethan?'

'He's here,' Harrison assured her. 'I have a three-year-old daughter and the two of them are talking. Can you hear them?'

There was so much noise going on around them, the general hustle and bustle of the shopping centre, the bad music played through the speakers, announcements, footsteps, crying babies, shopping carts being rattled about, but through all that Liv strained to hear her son talking to Yolanda.

'Oh, yeah? Well, *I've* got a new truck. That's better than your doll,' Ethan was saying, and Liv almost smiled with relief. Then the look on her face changed to one of pain again and she tensed, pushing once more. Amelia met Harrison's gaze, the unspoken communication between doctors working like a charm. The contractions were quite close.

'These aren't Braxton-Hicks.'

Amelia smiled.

The security man returned and Harrison was able to splint Liv's lower left leg. While he did that, Amelia fashioned a cervical collar from a few of the bandages in order to support Liv's neck when they moved her.

'Right. AJ. You support her head and neck. You…' he pointed to the security man '…support her legs. I'll support her body. Bring the stretcher in closer and someone clear a path to the room we're heading to. We don't need to be waiting for people to get out of the way. Mrs D.?'

'I've got the children,' she called from the side. 'Oh, and I'll take your bags for you, Amelia.'

'Thanks,' she answered, having forgotten about her shopping purchases. Thankfully, they were able to move Liv to a much more private environment without further complication. It was a small room with a bed, chair and washbasin. They left Liv on the stretcher rather than putting her onto the bed, not wanting to move her more than was necessary. Just outside the door was an area with chairs and a beverage machine, and a box of toys was in the corner. Down the hall were the management offices for the shopping centre. Liv had asked that her mother be called and the security man had quickly volunteered to take care of that. When they'd enquired after the baby's father, Liv had simply said he wasn't in the picture any more.

Mrs D. stayed outside with the children while Harrison and Amelia examined their patient once more. 'Liv?' Amelia called as she pulled on a pair of gloves. 'I'm going to do an internal, just to check how far you're dilated. All right?'

'Yes.'

They helped Liv remove her clothing, Harrison finding a blanket in the cupboard beneath the washbasin and placing that over their patient, more for modesty than anything else. 'Have you done many deliveries?' Harrison asked Amelia as he washed his hands.

'A few, but I haven't done one for a while.' She stood next to him, their voices barely above a whisper so they didn't alarm or upset their patient.

He grinned. 'It's like riding a bike. You take control of the delivery angle, I'll monitor Liv.'

Amelia nodded. 'Good.' She met his gaze and it was then she realised how close they were standing together. The room was by no means large so she would have to take care not to bump into him.

'Uh…' Harrison looked into her blue eyes, amazed at how deep the colour was. Every time he'd seen her during the past week at the hospital, he'd come to realise just how beautiful she really was, both inside and out. He'd also been curious to know what had upset her the afternoon she had come to his house for tea and biscuits, and today that brief flash of sadness in her face when Liv had reassuringly squeezed little Ethan's hand had given him a clue. Had she lost a child in the past? Was that it? It had to be something and it was a puzzle he was determined to somehow put together.

Amelia turned back to their patient, clearing her throat. 'Liv, did you have any back or stomach pain before coming to the shops today?' She crouched down and began the examination.

'A bit. I didn't sleep much last night but that's to be expected.'

'Did you simply lose your footing on the escalator or were you pushed?' Harrison asked as he rechecked her bandages.

'I…er…lost my footing, I guess.'

'You remember it all?'

Liv closed her eyes. 'Yes.'

'That's a good sign, then. No memory loss.'

'Do you remember your waters breaking?'

'What? No,' Liv replied, then gasped. 'I had a funny sensation in the shower this morning but I thought it was just loss of bladder control.'

'Did you feel heavier afterwards?'

'Yes, come to think of it.'

'Well, your waters have definitely broken because you're fully dilated,' Amelia announced. 'This baby is coming now.'

Liv tensed again as another contraction took hold of her body and she pushed again. She grabbed hold of Harrison's hand and squeezed it, but he didn't seem to mind. When the contraction finally subsided, she apologised to Harrison.

'That's all right. I've been on the receiving end before.'

Amelia watched as he smiled down at their patient, his voice reassuring and relaxing. Yes, she was sure he would have been very supportive to his wife during Yolanda's birth. He was such a doting father and she admired him for tackling the world of single parenthood, rather than leaving Yolanda's care to nannies. Sure, he had Mrs D. but from what Amelia had seen, the woman filled the role of grandmother and housekeeper. She was a part of their family unit, not just the hired help. Besides, she'd seen for herself the amazing relationship between father and daughter and was envious of the bond they shared.

Harrison glanced at her and Amelia immediately looked away, hoping he hadn't seen that wistful and longing expression on her face. She couldn't help her thoughts and the knowledge she could never have children, would never know what it was like to feel a life grow within her, was a part of her and something she lived with daily. She couldn't turn her emotions on and off like a tap, no matter how hard she tried.

'Oh, yes,' Liv said as she closed her eyes. 'You have a little girl.'

'See? Memory is definitely good.'

There was a pause, then Liv choked on a sob. 'The baby's not…? It's all right, isn't it?' A tear trickled down her cheek.

'It's not breech, if that's what you mean,' Amelia answered reassuringly as she did another check. 'In fact, I can see the head, so no problems on that side. Did you have a long labour last time?'

'Yes, and then ended up with an emergency Caesarean.'

'Second babies tend to deliver faster and also this one's probably had enough of being warm and cosy inside you. It wants to come out and join the fun.'

'When are you due?' Harrison asked, taking hold of Liv's hand as she groped for it yet again.

'Two more weeks.'

'Well, this one's impatient to make an entrance.'

'It was kicking so hard.' Liv ground the last few words out as she clenched her teeth and went with the flow of the contraction.

'That's it,' Harrison encouraged. 'Breathe. Remember to breathe.'

'You're doing well, Liv,' Amelia looked up and smiled. 'The head is coming.' When the contraction had eased, Amelia glanced at Harrison. 'Do you mind seeing when the ambulance will get here, please?'

He nodded and returned a moment later. 'About another five minutes.'

'Good. OK, Liv. When the next contraction comes, I want you to really concentrate on your pushing. I know it's difficult, I know you're uncomfortable, but you need to concentrate.'

'My head hurts.'

'We know,' Harrison said gently. 'Soon you can rest. Soon.' He was checking beneath the washbasin again and pulled out another blanket, opening it up and putting it on the chair. He looked into the medical kit and pulled out a pair of scissors, as well as some string, which he cut into suitable lengths so they could tie off the umbilical cord.

'Hand! I need to squeeze your hand,' Liv demanded, and Harrison was once more by her side as the next contraction came. Amelia had to admit she was impressed. Harrison was sweet, attentive and compassionate towards their patient. He had a reassuring bedside manner, which she knew was part of the reason Liv was able to stay calm. He chatted to her, encouraged her and turned on that charm of his.

She'd heard him checking on Mrs D. and the children when he'd gone to ask about the estimated time of arrival of the ambulance. He'd shared a few words with Ethan and was now telling Liv that her son was having fun playing trucks and tea parties with Yolanda. He also told her that her mother was on the way and that, too, seemed to calm Liv so she could cope with the delivery of her second child.

When Liv started to push again, Amelia shook her head, focusing her thoughts and getting them off Harrison. 'OK. That's it. That's it. Keep pushing,' she encouraged. 'One more and the head will be out. That's it.'

'Breathe,' Harrison reminded Liv.

Amelia held her own breath as she watched the baby's head finally come out. 'You've done it. Wonderful.' She reached her fingers around to check for the cord. 'Now, don't push. I just need to check.'

'But I need to,' Liv said.

'No.' Harrison's voice was clear and firm. 'Squeeze my hand. As hard as you can.' He watched Amelia's expression go from pleased to concerned in a split second and instinctively knew the cord was around the neck.

Her next words confirmed it. 'Don't push, Liv. The cord is around the neck. I'm going to try and unhook it.'

Liv was now panting, her gaze focused on Harrison who was helping her to control the very natural urge to push. 'I can't. I can't.'

'You can,' he said, and the words were filled with such assurance that even Amelia believed him.

'It's tight.' Amelia tried again, knowing she couldn't pull on the cord or she'd risk damaging the baby further. 'It won't move.' She racked her brains, knowing Liv would soon be overpowered by the urge to push.

'Cut it,' Harrison said.

'That's what I was thinking.' She reached over to where he'd prepared the pieces of string. 'Hold on, Liv. Just keep holding on. I'm going to do this as quickly as I can.' It was very slippery but Amelia managed to slip the pieces of string around the umbilical cord and tie them off as tightly as she could.

'I can't. I can't.'

'Almost.'

The urgency, the tension filled all three of them and at that moment the paramedics burst into the room.

'Get out!' Harrison ordered, his voice so fierce, they immediately retreated. Nothing could break the concentration, the link between the two doctors, their patient and the little baby whose life was in danger.

Amelia secured the last piece of string then reached for the scissors. 'All right. I'm cutting now, Liv. Just hang on.' She could feel the perspiration peppering her brow as she slid the scissors carefully around the cord, the baby's skin all covered in vernix.

The scissors weren't the sharpest ones around as they were more than likely used to cut bandages rather than hard, thick, rubbery umbilical cords, but finally she was through and the baby was free.

'Done,' was all she said, and took a moment to breathe. 'Shoulders are now rotating. Push when you're ready.'

When the next contraction came, Liv pushed and the shoulders were out. It took just one more push until a baby boy slid into Amelia's waiting hands. He was very slippery and she juggled him for a second, but Harrison was there in an instant, the blanket he'd prepared ready and waiting. Amelia placed the baby onto the blanket before he wrapped him up to keep the infant warm.

There was a little cry and all three adults in the room smiled at the sound. Never had Amelia heard anything more beautiful in her life, tears starting to sting her eyes as she glanced down at the baby. The miracle of life had a way of affecting everyone, but especially Amelia.

'You have a little boy,' Harrison told Liv as he carried the bundle over so she could see her son for the first time. Raising a shaking hand, Liv touched the baby's face, then dropped her hand and closed her eyes.

'He's gorgeous,' Amelia crooned, and sniffed. Harrison smiled, both of them captured in the moment, and in that instant she felt a bond form between them.

'Can I sleep now?' Liv said weakly, smiling at her new son.

'I think I'll get the paramedics in.' Amelia stood, wanting to pull herself together after seeing the way Harrison's deep brown eyes had grown rich with unspoken caring. He cared about her? No. Surely she was reading that wrong. She ripped off her gloves before tossing them in the bin, glancing down at her clothes and seeing the stains. She didn't care. If stained clothes were what it took to ensure the health and well-being of Liv and her son, then so be it. She opened the door and beckoned the paramedics in, apologising for kicking them out a few minutes before.

'Understandable,' the man said as he came into the room. 'Want me to deliver the afterbirth?'

'Be my guest.' Amelia crossed to Liv's side and

brushed a few loose strands of hair out of her patient's eyes. 'You did good.' She sniffed as she crossed to where Harrison was sitting on the seat, the baby on his knee as he checked him out.

'We can probably cut the cord a little shorter now. He's breathing just fine.'

'Sure.' She looked down at the crying baby. 'Nothing wrong with his lungs.' She turned to one of the paramedics. 'Do you have a pair of locking scissors I can use?'

'Of course.'

Amelia and Harrison dealt with the baby, placing a dressing over the rest of the cord before wrapping him up again to keep him warm.

'Do you want to hold him?' Harrison asked, holding the crying baby out to her.

Amelia knew she shouldn't, but she simply couldn't resist and held out her hands for him. The little mite was adorable and she smiled down at him. 'Hello there, handsome.'

He was opening his mouth, rooting around for something to suck on, and she walked to the sink, washed her little finger and placed it into his mouth. 'Good sucking reflex,' she said a moment later, and after a second he spat her finger out again and started to cry once more. She patted his bottom and crooned to him, trying to get him to quieten for a moment.

Harrison watched her and was overcome by how natural she seemed. It only strengthened his resolve that she may have once had a child of her own. The other thing he realised was that she looked highly desirable, standing there, holding a crying baby. It was ridiculous. Most men were attracted to fashionable women, not ones covered with stains, messy hair and holding a newborn, yet to him she looked…just right.

Amelia dragged in a deep breath, loving the feel of the small baby in her arms, but it did nothing to stop her from wishing that things had been different. She felt tears burn her eyes and she knew she had to get out of there, cursing her inability to hide her feelings. When she looked up she was surprised to find Harrison watching her.

'I need to get changed.' She gently placed the baby into his arms and rubbed at her eyes, pretending she was just tired. 'Just as well I went shopping earlier.' She knew her voice was shaky but she couldn't help it.

'Just as well,' he said, shifting the baby so one of his hands was free. He grabbed hers before she walked away. 'Hey. Good job, AJ.'

Amelia glanced down at their hands, surprised to find hers holding his equally as tight. It was strange to see her fingers linked with his and in that one moment she felt a strange sense of calm wash over her as she realised it was all right. It was all right for her to like someone…to like *him*.

His eyes were as dark as warmed chocolate and just as inviting when she looked into them, and she was faced with another revelation—Harrison was experiencing the same sensations she was. It wasn't just a figment of her imagination. Perhaps it was the birth that had made them both lower their defences.

'You, too,' she finally said, her voice barely above a whisper.

Harrison's lips lifted into a smile at her words and for some reason her heart seemed to pound even faster at the way this handsome, gorgeous man was looking at her. Puzzled and needing some space, she backed away, almost knocking into the paramedic. 'I'll...um... get changed.' She turned, opened the door and stepped out, closing it behind her. Mrs D. took one look at her and instantly held up the shopping bags.

'I think you'll be needing these,' she said, and Amelia accepted them with thanks. Yolanda and Ethan were playing on the floor but both stopped when she came out. Yolanda was the first one to her feet and with her hands on her hips, demanded, 'Is dat paint? I like painting.'

Amelia smiled. 'No, sweetie. This isn't paint.' The security man instantly pointed out the way to the nearest female restroom and, nodding her thanks, Amelia headed in that direction.

She wished she could shower as well but the change of clothes certainly did the trick and when she'd bundled her soiled clothing into one of the shopping bags, she stopped in front of the mirror and looked at her reflection.

'It's nothing,' she told herself. 'There's nothing special between the two of you. Just forget him. He's your boss. Nothing more. That moment you shared was because of the miracle of birth. That's all.' She splashed some cool water on her face, dabbed herself dry with the paper hand towel and finger-combed her hair.

'Amelia?'

She was startled when Mrs D. came into the restroom but she was instantly alert. 'Is there a problem?'

'No. No. The paramedics are ready to go.'

'Oh. OK. Thanks.' Amelia gathered up her things and they walked back to the little area where the children were playing. She put her bags down against the wall and went over to where Liv had been transferred to the paramedics' stretcher. 'How are you feeling?'

Liv smiled. 'Tired.'

'I understand. Has your mother arrived yet?'

'About a minute ago,' Harrison said, as he walked out of the room where they'd delivered the baby. Liv's mother was with him, cradling her new grandson. He took one look at Amelia and found it difficult not to stare. She'd changed her clothes and she looked stunning, the blue of her top changing her eyes to a deeper colour, and his gut tightened.

'You are coming to the hospital, aren't you?' Liv said, breaking the moment, and Harrison looked at their patient who was speaking to both doctors.

'Of course,' Amelia said.

Harrison nodded. 'See you there,' he said as the paramedics wheeled Liv away, Ethan and his grandmother following behind with the new baby. Now that it was just Harrison and his family, Amelia knew she had to extract herself once more and quickly picked up her bags.

'Mrs D.,' he said softly. 'Why don't you take Yolanda home while I head to the hospital with AJ? I shouldn't be long.'

'OK.' Mrs D. told Yolanda to pack up her toys but the girl wasn't having a bar of it.

'Daddy tum home, too.'

Harrison crouched down and touched his daughter's hair. 'Daddy needs to go to the hospital. Just for a little while.'

'No!' Yolanda stamped her foot. 'No. My daddy.'

'I don't think she liked seeing you hold that other baby,' Mrs D. said softly. Amelia just watched, knowing she was intruding and should probably leave but she found it impossible to move.

'I won't be long, pumpkin.'

'No, Daddy.' Tears instantly sprang to Yolanda's eyes and she flung herself into his arms. He cradled her tightly and picked her up as she cried on his shoulder.

'She's tired,' Mrs D. said. 'Come on, Yolanda. Daddy won't be long. You've been such a good girl, you can have a treat when you get home. You can watch your favourite show on TV and sing and dance and have lots of fun.'

'I want my daddy,' she said stubbornly, and Harrison was clearly torn.

'It's all right, Harrison,' Amelia said. 'I can do the check on Liv. Go home.'

'But I told Liv…'

'Liv has a three-year-old as well. She'll understand. Spend time with your family.'

Harrison knew the grown-up thing was to leave Yolanda with Mrs D. and quickly go to work to check on his patient. Yet he had promised Yolanda they'd spend the day together and if he left her now, it might cause more issues later.

As he looked at his beautiful daughter, who so badly needed him, it hit home just how pointless it was to even think about the attraction he felt for AJ. He'd been stunned when they'd shared that moment after the baby's birth, wondering if he'd been correct in reading the signals. Signals that he knew he should ignore.

He'd stayed away from relationships since Inga's death, not only because of Yolanda and not wanting to upset the routines he worked so hard to create, but also because he himself wasn't that good at trusting women. Inga had done a number on him and had left Yolanda scarred for life. He knew people couldn't see Yolanda's disability, it wasn't evident in her features, but mentally the child needed help and he was the only one who could provide it. He was her father. She needed him.

His mind made up, he nodded to Amelia. 'Thanks. I'll head home.'

'OK.' Amelia hesitated. 'I can…um…stop by on my way back from the hospital and give you an update, if you like?'

Harrison appreciated her thoughtful gesture as well as the opportunity to see her again but he quickly squashed it. 'It's fine. I can check it out at work on Monday.'

Amelia was a little disappointed but hid it well. 'Of course. Well, have a nice afternoon.'

'You, too. Don't stay too long at the hospital. Goodbye, Amelia-Jane,' he said, and walked out of the room, leaving Amelia with the impression that he'd been saying goodbye for good.

———

CHAPTER FOUR

AMELIA didn't sleep well that night, wondering if she'd done something wrong where Harrison was concerned. Although she couldn't help but like the man and his gorgeous little girl she knew the attraction between them couldn't go anywhere. Still, the way he'd said good-bye…it rankled and she didn't want her thoughts to be constantly disturbed with thoughts of him.

Amelia was rostered on for day shift and reported to work bright and early on Sunday morning, ready for whatever the day was going to throw at her. She'd pushed Harrison and his daughter to the back of her mind, closed the door and locked it—tight. At the end of June she would be leaving Australia and heading back to England and she needed to remain focused.

The steady Sunday morning trickle of patients was enough to keep her busy but just before lunch Rosie took a call from an ambulance on its way in. 'Oh, my goodness.' Rosie put the phone down, her hand resting on the receiver for a moment.

'What is it?' Amelia asked, and Rosie snapped back to reality.

'Ambulance is on its way in with Harrison's housekeeper. Apparently she fell and couldn't move. Suspected fractured hip.'

'Mrs Deveraux? Oh, poor woman.'

'That's the lady.' Rosie stood. 'I'll assist on this patient. Usually when it's a staff member's family or relative, the head of unit is called in.'

'That would be Harrison.' Amelia nodded and headed towards TR1. 'What's the ambulance ETA?'

'Five minutes.'

'Right. Where's that fancy new digital X-ray machine?'

'I'll organise it,' Rosie said.

'Page the head of orthopaedics and also head of anaesthetics. If she has fractured her hip, she may need a total hip replacement and Harrison's going to want it done as soon as possible.'

'I'll get it organised.'

'Get Mrs Deveraux's case notes ordered up. I want to know her blood type and anything she may be allergic to.'

Rosie headed off to instruct her nursing staff while Amelia checked everything in TR1, going over different scenarios in her head. Poor Mrs D. She wondered what had happened. Had Yolanda seen the fall? Was the little girl upset? Had Harrison been there or had he been out for a run along the beach?

When the ambulance siren came closer, Amelia headed out to meet it, not surprised when Harrison opened the doors from the inside and climbed out the second the vehicle stopped. 'Come here, pumpkin,' he said, turning and holding his arms out.

'No!' came the wail from Yolanda.

'It's all right.' Harrison soothed. Amelia walked over, noticing he was once more dressed in his painting garb. He looked so handsome, all scruffy like that.

'Hi,' she said, and peered into the back of the ambulance to see Yolanda clutching Mrs D., the chubby arms wrapped around the woman's hand. 'Oh, Yolanda. Did you come to see me at work?' she asked with delight, and the little girl looked up in surprise. Amelia noted the tear-stained face and realised Harrison must have already had a tough morning. Mrs D. was also trying to do her best to get Yolanda to let go. 'Why don't you come out with me and let the ambulancemen get Mrs D. out? Then you can use my stethoscope to listen to her heart because you're a good doctor.'

'I da doctor,' Yolanda said and slowly loosened her hold.

'You're an excellent doctor,' Harrison said, and held his hand out for his daughter once more, the paramedics waiting impatiently to get to their patient. There was no point in removing Yolanda by force or trying to get her out any sooner than necessary if he didn't want her to end up having a complete tantrum, which he was trying to avoid at all costs.

'Yes, remember how well you bandaged Daddy's hand the other day,' Amelia agreed, and Harrison could have hugged her. He had no idea how or why Yolanda had taken to Amelia, but the fact that she had was a godsend at this moment.

Amelia held out her stethoscope. 'Here you go, darling. You come and hold this while Mrs D. gets to ride on the wheely-bed inside.'

'I want a ride, too.'

Amelia glanced across at the porter standing by the door, looking on interestedly. 'Do you have a spare wheelchair I could borrow?' she asked.

'Sure.' He brought one over.

'I've got something better than the bed,' Amelia said with delight. 'I've got a wheely-chair.'

'Oh,' Mrs D. said with disappointment. '*I* wanted to ride in the chair not the bed. You're so lucky, Yolanda.'

Instantly, the child released the woman and headed for her father, who lifted her from the ambulance and into the waiting wheelchair. Amelia handed over her stethoscope and the child took it eagerly, hooking it into her ears and listening to her heartbeat like a pro.

'I see she's done that before.' Amelia smiled at Harrison.

'Thank you.' His words were soft but the look in his eyes was totally heartfelt.

'No problem.' She pushed the wheelchair into the hospital.

'Tumming froo,' Yolanda called loudly, and several people turned to look, smiling at the picture they saw. 'Det out of da way,' she said crossly to a nurse. Amelia set the wheelchair to the side of TR1 and held out her hand to Yolanda.

'Come on. Let's see how Mrs D. is doing.' Pleased that Yolanda accepted her hand, they went to where Mrs D. was being transferred onto the hospital barouche. 'See? She's all right.'

'I listen,' Yolanda said, with her stethoscope ready.

'Listen to my heart first,' Amelia suggested, noting they weren't quite ready. She crouched down and let Yolanda do her doctor routine, all the while listening to Harrison explaining what had happened and then giving orders as to what he wanted. Apparently, Mrs D. had slipped in the kitchen and fallen hard.

'Stick tongue out,' Dr Yolanda instructed, and Amelia

obliged. 'Say, "Ah."' Again, Amelia did as she was told. 'You O-tay. Now Mrs D.'

'OK but I'll need to pick you up.'

Yolanda immediately held out her arms and Amelia lifted her, holding her close for a moment and breathing in the sweet scent of powder, sunshine and innocence. Delicious. When the blonde ringlets brushed the side of her face, Amelia smiled and couldn't help but drop a kiss on the flaxen head.

'All right, bring her over, AJ,' Harrison said. Although he'd been dealing with his housekeeper and making sure she was all right, he'd been watching and marvelling at the way Amelia had dealt with Yolanda. Was she good with all children or was it just his daughter? The two had certainly formed a bond, which, given that Amelia wasn't going to be here for very long, he wasn't sure was a good thing.

Amelia held Yolanda as she listened to Mrs D.'s heart and then made her stick her tongue out.

'Ooh, dat tongue not good. You need op-ray-shun.'

'She's good,' Rosie said with a chuckle.

'What do you expect?' Harrison preened. 'She's a chip off the old block. I just wish I could diagnose someone just by looking at their tongue.'

'Would save us all a lot of time,' Amelia agreed. 'Dr Yolanda, do you think we need to take some X-rays?'

Yolanda thought for a moment. 'Yes. X-rays now.' With that, she wriggled out of Amelia's arms and all but tossed her stethoscope back at her, Amelia catching it just in time. 'I do da witing now.'

'I'll take her,' one of the nurses said, but Yolanda flatly refused, clinging to Amelia's hand.

'No. I stay Meel-ya.'

Amelia was filled with pride and pleasure at the acceptance from the three-year-old. Never before had she become this close to a child and it was…lovely. 'We'll go to the nurses' station and write up the notes,' she said, and again Harrison nodded.

'I'll let you know when we have an image.' Harrison smiled at her, then winked. Amelia headed off with Dr Yolanda in tow, trying to control the warm and fuzzy feeling he'd given her by winking. She wished he hadn't done it because winking was intimate, personal and it only served to enhance the connection she felt with him.

She sat Yolanda next to her at the nurses' station, giving her a piece of paper and a pen. The little girl began writing, mumbling to herself as she made important squiggles on the page. Amelia listened to her, recognising 'tongue' and 'op-ray-shun' as she continued her earnest reporting.

When Harrison came to get her, Yolanda was still very busy. Amelia smiled at him. 'Do you mumble when you write up notes?' she asked, and watched as he shrugged with slight embarrassment.

'I might,' he said slowly, then chuckled. 'We have an image.'

'What's the verdict?'

'Come and see. Yolanda? Do you want to see the X-ray?' he asked, and she stopped her 'work' and went willingly into his arms. The three of them headed back to TR1.

'The fact that you're not looking so stressed must mean it's good news,' Amelia commented.

'It's better than I'd hoped,' Harrison replied, surprised she'd been able to read him so easily.

Amelia looked at the digital image they'd captured and nodded. 'Excellent. Acetabula cup is intact, the head of the femur looks good. Mrs D., you've fractured the neck of femur in just the right place. Any higher and you would have needed a total hip replacement.'

'That's what Harrison said.'

'And me, too,' Yolanda demanded, trying to touch the digital screen, but her father kept pulling her hand back.

'You're the best little doctor,' he said, kissing her cheek.

'I a *big* doctor.'

'Yes, of course. I'm sorry.'

The orthopaedic surgeon arrived and Amelia offered to take Yolanda again while Harrison spoke to him, but this time Yolanda chose to stay with her father.

'The break is easily fixed with a few screws, possibly a plate if we need it, but for the most part surgery should take about forty-five minutes,' the orthopod reported.

'What time can you get her in?' Harrison asked, and the surgeon checked what time Mrs D. had last eaten.

'I'd say around three this afternoon.'

Harrison nodded. 'Great.' He shook hands with the orthopod and the anaesthetist, leaving Mrs D. in their hands.

'Are you heading home now?' Amelia asked as they walked back to the nurses' station.

'No. I think we'll hang around.'

'That's a long time to hang around,' she said, glancing at Yolanda, who'd scrambled out of her father's arms and resumed her medical reporting, adding another sheet of paper. 'Won't Yolanda get bored?'

'No. She's used to the hospital. Besides, I think she'd like to go to the zoo.'

Amelia frowned. 'I thought you were going to stay—'

At the word 'zoo', Yolanda had stopped what she'd

been doing, her face filled with delight. 'Zoo! Zoo!' She clambered off the chair and started jumping around, clapping her hands.

'I think I'm missing something,' Amelia said. 'The zoo's in the city, isn't it?'

Harrison took Yolanda's hand. 'Why don't we show AJ the zoo?' he asked his daughter, who immediately nodded and slipped her other hand into Amelia's, putting herself between the two adults. 'Let's go.'

They headed down the corridor to the lifts, Yolanda running ahead to press the button. 'I do it,' she said, and when the lift arrived, she pressed the button for the fourth floor.

'They have a zoo in the hospital? Isn't that against health regulations?'

Harrison smiled. 'It's what she calls the children's ward because there are animals all around the playroom and there's a gate that keeps all the live little animals…' he tickled his daughter as he said the words '…safe inside.'

'Oh. I haven't had a chance to see the children's ward yet.'

'That's why we brought you along.' When the lift arrived on the fourth floor, Yolanda was out like a shot and running down the corridor. Harrison quickened his pace but knew exactly where he'd find his daughter.

'She certainly knows her way around.'

'As I said, she's used to the hospital and she's been to the children's ward many times before.'

'Oh. Was she sick?'

Harrison considered the question for a moment. 'Not healthwise. She has regular appointments here, though.' He didn't have time to say anything else as Yolanda was standing by the gate into the 'zoo' and begging to be let in. He unlatched it and she rushed in, ignoring the other four children who were in there and headed straight for the soft animal toys.

'I'll just go speak to the sister, let her know Yolanda's here.' He disappeared and Amelia watched the little girl, noting the look of absolute delight on her face as she began pulling out one soft animal after another and lining them all up, talking to each of them in turn. When Harrison returned, he went in, holding the gate for Amelia who hesitantly followed.

'All right, pumpkin,' he said. 'You stay here until Daddy comes to get you.'

'O-tay.'

'What does she do if she needs you sooner?' Amelia asked.

Harrison turned to his daughter. 'What do you do, Yolanda, if you need Daddy?'

'I get da zoo-teeper and she get Daddy.' Yolanda nodded with satisfaction and accepted a kiss from her father before going back to bossing the animals around.

'I presume the zoo-keeper is the ward sister?' Amelia asked as they left Yolanda.

'Correct, Dr Watson.'

They headed back to A and E and Harrison went off to check on Mrs D. Rosie had another case for Amelia and she collected the notes and went to cubicle four to investigate. Two hours later, she was writing up a different set of case notes when another ambulance arrived.

The patient was wheeled in, yelling and screaming abuse at the staff. Amelia headed over, glad the paramedics had prewarned them about this one.

'June?' Amelia said, looking at the woman's large, pregnant belly. 'June, you need to calm down.'

The woman let go with a string of curses and the alcohol on her breath was both stale and putrid. 'Leave me alone. I don't have to do anything. I want to go. You can't make me stay.' As she spoke, she clutched her heart and Amelia immediately hooked her stethoscope into her ears.

'Let me listen, June.'

'Get away—'

'What is going on here?' Harrison demanded so loudly he made Amelia jump. 'You are disturbing my A and E department. Let Dr Watson examine you.'

His presence momentarily startled the woman and Amelia took the opportunity to listen to the woman's heart.

'It's rapid. Get a blood test, check her alcohol levels. There's swelling of the fingers.' She placed her fingers around June's ankles. 'Swelling there, too. I'll need a urine sample and get the obstetrics registrar here, stat. Possible pre-eclamptic patient.'

June again let her mouth run foul. 'You can't…get away—'

'She's irrational due to the alcohol,' Harrison said as one of the nurses tried to take June's blood pressure. Amelia noted a hardness to his tone she'd never heard before. 'Don't give her anything until the obstetrics registrar has seen her. Get a social worker here, stat. And while we're waiting…' he glared at June '…I think you need a little lesson on the detrimental effects of alcohol on your unborn child.'

June spat at him but missed.

'Charming. Just so you know, your current condition is serious. Both you and your baby could die due to the amount of alcohol you've poured into your body. If your baby doesn't die, it will be subjected to birth abnormalities. That means a high probability of facial deformities, growth retardation and brain abnormalities. All this *just* so you could have a good time and drink yourself stupid.' Although his voice had been soft, the hardness remained and Amelia realised there was more going on here than a thoughtless patient. Thankfully June had settled a bit while Harrison had been talking and the staff had been able to do the tests they needed. When the obstetrics registrar arrived, Amelia handed over June's care and grabbed Harrison's arm, tugging him from the treatment room.

'I'm going on my break now,' she called to the sister. Still holding his arm, she headed for the A and E tearoom, thankful it was empty. 'Are you all right?' she asked, closing the door behind them.

Harrison walked away from her, rubbing a hand over his face before raking it through his hair. 'It just gets me so mad.'

'I can see that.'

'She has no idea what she's done to her baby.'

Amelia took in his agitation, listened to the fury in his voice and realised there was much more to this than she'd initially thought. 'I brought you in here because I thought you needed to cool off. I still do, but if you feel like talking, getting something off your chest, then I'm more than happy to listen.'

Harrison paced around the room a few more times, shaking his head.

'This is personal, isn't it?' she finally said, and he stopped moving and looked at her. 'Yolanda?'

Harrison nodded. 'Yes. Yolanda.'

'That's what's wrong with her?'

He sighed. 'Short version first—when Yolanda was

born, she was suffering from alcohol withdrawal. When she was twelve months old, she was diagnosed under the foetal alcohol syndrome disorder banner. She has ARND.'

CHAPTER FIVE

'OH.' AMELIA was shocked. She wasn't sure what she'd been expecting him to say but it hadn't been that.

'Do you know what that is?'

'Alcohol-related neurodevelopmental disorder.' She nodded. 'I know about it but I've never dealt with it before.'

'Unfortunately, FASD is becoming more common. Like June out there. Goodness knows what she's doing to her baby.'

'It's not right.'

'You've got that straight, AJ.'

Amelia's pager sounded and she sighed, wishing they hadn't been interrupted. She checked the number. 'Orthopaedics. I'd say this is about Mrs D.' She crossed to the house phone and called.

'Is Harrison with you?' the surgeon asked.

'Yes.'

'We weren't sure how to contact him but triage sister said he was with you.'

Amelia held the phone out to Harrison. 'It's for you.'

He nodded and accepted the phone, listening for a moment. 'I'll be right there.'

'Problem?' she asked as he hung the receiver up and headed for the door.

'They're taking her in earlier and I wanted to see her.'

'Of course.' Amelia's pager sounded again and she rolled her eyes. 'Let me know what happens.'

'I will.' He paused at the door and looked at her. 'Thanks for listening, AJ.'

She smiled. 'I don't think I did much.'

'You'd be surprised.' With that he headed off and it took Amelia a moment to get her thoughts in gear before returning to her job. Now this day was really starting to drag.

Mrs Deveraux's operation went well and even though Amelia's shift had finished, she waited around until the housekeeper was in Recovery.

'You still here?' Harrison asked as she came into Recovery.

'Yes. Yolanda still at the zoo?'

He nodded. 'I've just received a call from the ward sister.'

'You mean zoo-keeper,' she corrected him, and he smiled. 'How's Mrs D.?'

'Doing well. Surgery was uncomplicated and she'll only have to be in hospital for about five days.'

'I'll bet that's better than you initially thought.'

Harrison exhaled slowly. 'I heard her scream and then rushed into the kitchen to see her lying on the floor.' He shook his head. 'Her hip was at such a bad angle, I was positive she'd need a total hip replacement. Then Yolanda came in, took one look at Mrs D. and burst into tears.'

'Well, every thing's settled now.'

'Yes. I'd better go get Yolanda. Are you on your way home?'

'I am, thank goodness.'

'Want to walk together?'

Amelia smiled, tingles spreading through her. 'I'd love to.'

'Good. I'll meet you out front in about ten minutes.'

'Absolutely.' She watched as he headed off and then turned to Mrs Deveraux. A moment later, the house-keeper's eyes fluttered open. 'Hi, there.' Amelia smiled.

'It's over?' Mrs D. asked.

'You're all done. All fixed up and ready for a relaxing week eating hospital food and being put through your paces by physiotherapists.'

'That doesn't sound relaxing.' Mrs D. tried to laugh but her mouth was too dry. Amelia quickly scooped some ice chips for her. 'Thank you, dear.' She swallowed them and sighed. 'A whole week, you say?'

'Around five days. Hospitals usually like to kick patients out at Easter and that starts this coming Friday.'

'Oh dear. How will Harrison cope with Yolanda?'

Amelia admitted the thought had crossed her mind but she'd told herself firmly it was none of her business. 'He'll cope. He's resourceful.'

'But she can't go into daycare. It's not good for her. The other children won't understand and…' Mrs D. was starting to get worked up and Amelia immediately calmed her down.

'Shh. Harrison will sort it out. It'll be fine. Yolanda will be fine. You concentrate on getting better.'

'Yes.' Mrs D. closed her eyes. 'Yes.'

She was dozing once more when Amelia left to go and meet Harrison and Yolanda, and as they walked home, preferring to walk along the beach rather than the footpath, Amelia wondered whether she should ask him.

For the moment they were both content to watch Yolanda running ahead, looking at the shells on the sand, stopping every now and then to pick one up and put it in her pocket. 'Where does she get the energy?' Amelia asked. 'I'm getting exhausted just watching her.'

Harrison chuckled. 'She has healthy food prepared for her, she sleeps for hours a day…not all in one go, you understand. Two hours here, five hours there,' he added. 'And she doesn't have a care in the world. She's free.'

Amelia sighed. 'Sounds lovely, doesn't it?'

'We had it once.'

'Why did we let it go?'

'Innocence.' Harrison agreed with a nod. 'And Yolanda had part of her innocence taken away the instant she was born.'

'ARND?'

'Yes. I gave you the short version before. Are you ready for the long, extended one where you get all my footnotes and if you're lucky I might even draw you some pie graphs in the sand?'

Amelia chuckled. 'You seem OK with it all.'

'I am—*now*. It's been a long and difficult two years, AJ. Why women think it's OK to drink during pregnancy is totally beyond me. It's like driving a car without your seat belt on. It's common sense not to drink, that the alcohol will damage the baby, and yet they do it.'

'Women like June.' Amelia nodded in understanding.

'Seeing her just triggered the helplessness I first experienced when Yolanda was diagnosed. Inga probably drank throughout her entire pregnancy. Even when I eventually found out, she didn't stop.'

Amelia stayed silent, waiting for him to continue, knowing how important this was to him.

'She became pregnant with Yolanda almost immediately after we married, and for that first year things were a little rocky but workable. Six months after Yolanda's birth, she'd had enough of motherhood. She said she wanted a divorce and I was happy to go along with it. She moved out, into a hotel.'

'And you became a single father.'

'Yes. Inga had a drinking problem but she couldn't see it. I think she had a romantic picture of what it was like to be a doctor's wife.'

'You mean the money, the prestige, the big house and fancy cars?'

'All that and more. Instead, she was alone a lot of the time because I was always at the hospital. She hated the phone ringing on my days off and if I offered to cover for a friend or change with someone, she became livid.'

'Sounds like a bad time.'

'The bottle became her friend, along with other *special* friends, but that wasn't really until after Yolanda was born.'

'Yolanda is gorgeous, Harrison. You should be proud.'

'Thanks, AJ. I am but, gorgeous or not, the poor baby has suffered from having two parents who didn't do enough for her when it counted.'

'Did you try to stop your wife from drinking?'

'Once I found out, yes. Nothing seemed to work. She told me she'd stopped when she hadn't but, again, I wasn't around much.'

'You're a doctor, Harrison. It's your job.'

'My daughter's life and well-being should have been more important,' he argued. 'It's been a long and difficult road for me to admit my daughter has a disability and I'm part of the cause.'

'You're not the cause, Harrison. You're her hope.'

'I'm her *father*. I should have done more.'

'You're doing more now. What happened after she was diagnosed with ARND?'

'I sought help. I've managed to find a therapist who specialises in this area and she's been wonderful. She's helped me to realise that Yolanda is Yolanda and while she might do things differently from other children, she's my child and it's my responsibility to help her. I've realised that it's the parent who needs the most training. Once we can understand and adapt to the way our children do things, it makes life a lot easier all around.'

'You said she often wanders off.'

'Yes. Sometimes I feel like putting a chain of bells around her so I know where she is at all times.'

Amelia laughed. 'I think a lot of parents probably feel that way.'

'You could be right but she stops my heart every time I can't find her.'

Amelia watched the way he was rubbing his hands together, watching the agitation he was feeling. 'It was a good thing she was diagnosed so early.'

'I was almost waiting for the signs. As you can tell, she has no physical disability, no facial anomalies, no growth retardation. She does, however, have problems with her central nervous system but, again, they're not excessive. She has impaired fine motor skills and poor eye-hand co-ordination.'

'And yet she does baking with Mrs D.'

Harrison smiled. 'Part of her therapy.'

'And she gets to have fun, too.'

'Yes. She also has cognitive abnormalities, such as lower intellectual function and behaviour and social problems.'

'Not sleeping well at night? Wandering off?'

'Exactly, although her memory appears to be improving at the moment so that's a promising sign.'

'Oh. Has she had a breakthrough?'

'Yes. With you.'

'Me?' Amelia was astonished. 'How?'

'She's remembered you. You must have made a big impact on her because she's always asking when "Meelya" is coming back to play dolls.'

'Wow. I'm…I'm flattered.'

'Good. You should be.' He paused. 'In fact, she's quite taken with you, AJ.'

Amelia glanced at him, hearing the concern in his tone, and it took a moment for his words to sink in. 'Oh. That's perhaps not so good.'

'I think it's important to be honest with her, to let her know that you won't always be around.'

'Agreed.' Amelia looked ahead to where Yolanda had bent to pick up another shell before she came hurtling back to show them what she'd found. Her heart twisted with love and she realised she was already strongly attached to the little girl, but how could she not be? Yolanda was so easy to love.

And what of her father?

The thought simply popped into her head and Amelia tried to push it away. There could never be anything but friendship between herself and Harrison, even if she secretly wanted more. Suffering from endometriosis at such a young age hadn't been her idea of fun. It also meant she needed to be very choosy in her relationships with men and although she didn't have too much experience, it was more for self-preservation than fear of wanting to commit.

'OK,' Harrison was saying to his daughter. 'Find three more shells and then it's time to go home.'

Amelia glanced around them as Yolanda ran off again and she realised they were almost level with their respective homes. 'So…what are you going to do while Mrs Deveraux is in hospital?'

'Well, I'm not a bad cook, and the cleaning shouldn't be too difficult to maintain.'

Amelia laughed, tapping his shoulder lightly. 'That's not what I meant.'

Harrison smiled but it didn't last for long. 'Yolanda?' He shook his head. 'I've been trying to figure out the best solution. There's a daycare centre at the hospital but I'm not sure if they'd be able to take her at such short notice.'

'Would she be all right in daycare?'

'With the staff or the other children?'

'Both, but more so the children. Yolanda has the disadvantage of not *looking* as though she has a disability. Other children would expect her to react to things the same way they do.'

'It's only for a few days. I can take a day or so off.'

'Use up your annual leave? But you've just returned from a conference.'

'I know, and I'm behind in my paperwork, although I guess I could try and do that from home.'

Amelia thought for a moment, wondering whether she should say what was on the tip of her tongue. She cleared her throat. 'Well…um…I could help.'

Harrison turned to look at her. 'What?'

'I live close. Yolanda likes me. You could alter my shifts, put me on afternoons. That way, I'm with her when you leave in the morning and I can bring her to work with me in the afternoon when I start my shift.'

He pondered her offer for a moment, wondering whether he was capable of completely trusting Yolanda to Amelia's care. Could *he* trust Amelia? He'd trusted once and it had ended up with Yolanda suffering for that misplaced trust. So far, though, Amelia hadn't given him any reason not to trust her and Yolanda went to her without hesitation. Surely that was good? 'You'd be starting work at around three o'clock. The earliest I could leave would be around four-thirty,' he said out loud as he tried to work things through.

'The zoo?'

'Possibly. Yolanda has therapy three times a week. Well, Friday's out because that's a public holiday for Easter, so that leaves two sessions.'

'What time does she usually have them?'

'Around ten-thirty, but if I could change it to three o'clock, when you start work, then she could have her sessions and then go to the children's ward until I'm finished.' He nodded. 'That might just work, AJ.'

'What days does she have therapy?'

'Monday and Wednesday this week.'

'Well, my rostered day off is Tuesday—'

'And I'll take Thursday off.'

'And then it's just Friday, and Mrs D. should be ready to come home.'

'I'll still need help once Mrs D.'s home, but not as much.'

Amelia shrugged. 'I can still help.'

Harrison stopped walking and looked at her. 'That's really generous of you, AJ.'

Amelia shrugged again. 'Hey, that's what neighbours are for.'

'I'm very picky about who I leave my daughter with

but the way she goes to you, the way she trusts you, it speaks volumes.'

'And once Mrs D.'s up and about, I'll start backing off and spending less time with Yolanda. Sort of wean her off so when I leave at the end of June, she'll be…' Amelia's voice trailed off and she sighed.

'Sorry to see you go,' Harrison finished. 'She won't be the only one.' He reached for her hand and gave it a little squeeze and Amelia felt the heat from his touch warm her whole body. 'Thank you for offering to help.'

'You are going to take it, aren't you? I mean, it's the best thing for Yolanda.'

Harrison nodded and dropped her hand at the same time. 'I'm going to take your offer, yes.'

'Well…good.' Now that she'd made it and he'd accepted, she was starting to have second thoughts. She took in their surroundings. 'I'd…uh…better get going.' She jerked her thumb over her shoulder towards her apartment.

'Me, too. What were you rostered on to work tomorrow?'

'Nights. Tina's on afternoons so I'll call her to swap tomorrow and then we just need to sort out a swap for Wednesday—I was on a day shift.'

Harrison nodded. 'I'll do that tomorrow.'

'Thanks.' She headed off then stopped. 'I almost forgot, what time do you want me?'

His gaze widened. 'Pardon?'

'Uh…to report for duty in the morning,' she added quickly, realising the double-entendre.

'How's seven-thirty?'

'Great.' She started up the beach again, stopping to say goodbye to Yolanda on the way. The child gave her a shell and was then happy to part, and as Amelia walked quickly to her apartment, she knew she'd treasure the gift for ever.

Once safe behind the door of her apartment, she crossed to the phone and tapped out Tina's number. After four rings the answering-machine began its recorded message and Amelia growled down the phone.

'I'm here, I'm here,' Tina said, and switched the machine off. 'Who's growling at me?'

'It's *me*,' Amelia said.

'Oh, hey, there. How's life?'

'Miserable. You'll never guess what I've gone and done.'

'Do I need to get comfortable?'

'Very.' Amelia blurted out everything to her friend. 'And then I find myself offering to look after his daughter!'

Tina chuckled.

'What's so funny?' she demanded.

'I love the way you go to extraordinary lengths to keep yourself apart from people, to not get involved in people's lives, and here you're slap-bang in the middle of a relationship before you know it.'

'Relationship?'

'Yes, Amelia, or should I call you AJ?' Tina teased. 'You and Harrison. I've seen the way you two look at each other.'

'But I hardly know the man.'

'You're going to get to know him much better after the coming week.'

Amelia groaned. 'Perhaps I should go and tell him I can't help. I mean, you're right. I go to such lengths not to involve myself because happy families aren't for me. It's not healthy for me because I so desperately want to have a family but can't. It just isn't fair,' she wailed.

'That's very true.' Tina cleared her throat. 'But think about it this way, Amelia. You can't have kids and so even if you do find a gorgeous, handsome man and get married, you'll never have the happy children fantasy.'

'Your point?'

'You've just been given an opportunity.'

'I don't follow.'

'To play happy families. For the next few days you get to spend time with Yolanda. You get to be a mother figure to her. You know it can't last. You've told me that once Mrs D. is back on her feet you'll start withdrawing into your shell once more, so why not take this opportunity, Amelia?'

'It's cruel.'

'For who?'

'For me. It'll give me a taste of what I can never have.'

'It'll also give you one or two glorious weeks of heaven, especially if you and Harrison get closer.'

'Stop.' Amelia sighed. 'I guess it's too late to back out now.'

'Especially as I've already agreed to switch shifts with you.'

'You think I should do this?'

'I do.'

So Amelia-Jane Watson reported for duty to her boss's house at seven-thirty the next morning. Harrison opened the door and ushered her in. 'Sorry. I'm running late and I can't get Yolanda to eat her breakfast.'

She nodded and followed him through to the kitchen, where Yolanda was sitting up at the bench, a bowl of cereal, a plate of toast, a boiled egg, milk, juice and water sitting in front of her.

'She keeps changing her mind but I can't seem to get her to eat more than one mouthful and she's refusing to drink.'

Amelia tried to hide her smile at the mess but Harrison caught her.

'Don't you dare,' he said, pointing his finger.

'Sorry.' She covered her mouth with her hand but noticed his own lips twitching. 'Look, you head to the hospital, I'll try and get something into her.'

'No biscuits until she's eaten at least one of those,' he said to Yolanda, pointing to the food in front of his daughter. 'Daddy's got to go to the hospital.'

'Landa tum, too.' She started climbing off the stool but he stopped her.

'No, pumpkin. Daddy gets to go to *boring* work but you get to stay here and play *dolls* with *Amelia*. You lucky duck.'

Yolanda thought about that for a moment. 'Yay. I lucky duck.'

'OK. Kiss Daddy.' She did. 'Drink your juice.' She didn't. Harrison snapped his fingers and shrugged. 'I just can't win.'

Amelia laughed as he started putting papers into his briefcase. 'How's Mrs D. this morning?'

'She's doing well. I'll stop by and see her and if there's any change I'll give you a call, but I'm expecting her to make an uncomplicated recovery.' He glanced around him. 'Where are my car keys?'

Amelia looked on the kitchen bench and saw a set of keys. She picked them up and dangled them from her finger. 'These?'

'Ah. AJ. You're brilliant.' He snagged the keys and then headed for the door. 'I'm taking the car today so call me if you need anything or if there's any trouble. Keep the doors locked while you're in the house as she's as slippery as an eel.'

'Noted. Go.' She watched him walk out, realising they'd just played out a perfect domestic scene… except for the ending. The ending was usually where the husband kissed the wife before leaving for work. At least, that was the way it worked in the stereotypical world. Even the thought of Harrison kissing her, and she'd thought about it on quite a few occasions, was enough to make her feel hot and cold all over.

When his car had disappeared down the driveway, she made sure the door was locked and returned to Yolanda's side. The child was still sitting at the bench but the food was now smothered and smeared all over the kitchen bench, the cup of juice dripping down the sides and onto the floor.

'Perfect domestic scene,' Amelia muttered to herself before she set about getting things cleaned up. The two of them had a good day and she even managed to get both food and drink into Yolanda, but the cherry on top was when the child gave way to sleep after lunch and dozed in the lounge for a good hour and a half.

Amelia picked up the phone and called Harrison at the hospital. 'Hi. It's me,' she said.

'Hey. I was just about to call you.'

'I figured as much as it's almost an hour since your last call.'

'Oh. I haven't been calling too much, have I?'

'Hourly check-ups might be considered a bit much

but it's the first day so I'm letting it slide. Try it tomorrow and you might get a different story.'

Harrison chuckled. 'Sorry. Over-protective father and all that.'

'I understand,' she said, letting the sound of his laughter wash over her. 'Anyway, I just wanted to let you know I've managed to get her to sleep and didn't want you ringing in case the phone woke her.'

'Good going.' He was impressed.

'We'll see you around three o'clock.'

'Looking forward to it,' he said, and rang off.

Amelia settled back next to Yolanda, her hand resting on the child's head. She'd known the little girl would be a lot of work but the morning had been very full. Not that she hadn't enjoyed it—she had. They'd both had a ball, playing dolls and dancing in front of the television and having tea parties, but she had to go to work soon and somehow stay awake. She was glad the next day was her rostered day off.

Just after half past two they packed a bag for Yolanda, stopped at Amelia's apartment so she could quickly change for work and then set out, walking along the beach towards the hospital. Yolanda managed to collect two pocketfuls of shells and by the time they arrived at the hospital Amelia had to stop and brush all the sand off the three-year-old before presenting her to her father.

'Here she is. All in one piece.'

Harrison gave Yolanda a big cuddle then looked at Amelia. 'Can't say the same for you. You look a little frazzled, Dr Watson.'

'I feel it. How does Mrs D. do it?'

'Ah, that's elementary, my dear Watson. She doesn't

have to come and work a shift at the hospital after spending all day running around after an active three-year-old.'

'I guess. I think I even slept for half an hour while Yolanda was sleeping, I was so worn out.'

Harrison chuckled. 'That's what wise parents do. Now, if you'll excuse me, I'll get Yolanda up to her therapy appointment.'

Amelia nodded, pleased with his reference to wise parents, and she hugged herself. She may be exhausted but she'd had an amazing time playing with Yolanda and she couldn't thank Harrison enough for giving her the opportunity to play happy families for a few days. Tina was right. This might be good for her.

Tuesday panned out much the same only this time Amelia not only knew what to expect but had better control over things. She was even able to cook dinner for Harrison so by the time he returned home from the hospital, a little later than usual, she was just taking a pasta bake out of the oven.

'Something smells good,' he said, as he scooped up Yolanda and came into the kitchen. Again, it was a domestic scene and Amelia could once more imagine him coming over and giving her a kiss.

'I'm…uh…no chef but I can get by.'

Harrison chuckled and let a squirming Yolanda go. 'Had a better day?' he asked, picking up a fork and digging it into the steaming dish.

'Hey. Just wait and I'll dish it up onto a plate for you.'

'Thanks. I'm ravenous.'

'There's a salad in the fridge so why don't you get that out? I've also made Yolanda's favourite.' She opened the microwave door and retrieved a bowl of porridge.

'Porridge? That's her favourite?'

'It is today. She's eaten three bowls of it and also demanded it for dinner.'

'A bit repetitive but, hey, she's eating and it's healthy.' Harrison nodded. 'Good work, Watson.'

'Thanks, Stapleton.' She took out one plate and started dishing up.

'Wait. Aren't you having any?'

'Uh…I…er…no.'

'Why not? There's plenty here and it seems ridiculous for you to go back to your apartment and cook. No. Stay and we can have dinner.'

She shrugged, knowing it was pointless to argue, and pulled out another plate. Harrison sat Yolanda down and watched with delight as she dug into the porridge.

'I've never seen her eat so well. Amelia-Jane, you're a miracle-worker.'

She blushed with pleasure at his compliments. The three of them sat at the kitchen bench and ate dinner together, Harrison keeping the conversation flowing on a light level. After he'd seen Amelia to the door and said goodnight, he concentrated on getting his daughter settled. Thankfully, it didn't take long and while he sat by her bed, stroking her blonde curls, he thought about Amelia and how tempting it had been to simply walk into the house, cross to Amelia's side and kiss her.

It felt natural and right and that alone should be scaring him…but it wasn't. He'd had one bad marriage, yes, but it didn't take a fool to notice that Amelia-Jane Watson was completely different from his ex-wife. For starters, Yolanda adored her 'Meel-ya' and he'd often relied on Yolanda's inbuilt radar, believing that kids could sense the goodness in a person.

He walked into the kitchen and began clearing away

the dishes, rinsing them before stacking them in the dishwasher, and once he was done he settled down to do some paperwork. Five minutes later he crossed to the TV and turned it on. Two minutes later he turned it off and started to pace around, wondering what was wrong with him. Amelia-Jane was on his mind and along with thoughts of her came thoughts of kissing her, and he realised the urge to press his mouth to hers was intensifying faster than he'd anticipated.

Also, for some inexplicable reason, his house felt all wrong. Perhaps it was because Mrs D. wasn't around but after a moment he dismissed that thought. It was Amelia. For the past two days she'd been there, caring for his daughter, and somehow she'd put her stamp on the place. She hadn't rearranged anything, nothing had outwardly changed, but when he walked into the kitchen he could smell her perfume. When he looked at Yolanda's room, he pictured Amelia and his daughter, side by side, playing dolls. Thoughts of her, visions of her were all around his house and it felt…right.

It also made him feel lonely, and until that moment it was a feeling he hadn't thought he'd ever experience.

CHAPTER SIX

WEDNESDAY was a repeat of Monday, the only thing different being the overwhelming urge to kiss Harrison hello and goodbye whenever she saw him. Amelia was glad when Thursday came and it was Harrison's turn to stay at home and look after his daughter. Amelia caught up with Mrs Deveraux at the hospital, pleased to see the housekeeper up and about.

'I can go home tomorrow,' she told Amelia the instant she saw her.

'That's fantastic news.'

'Yes, and thank you, dear, so much for helping Harrison and Yolanda.'

Amelia smiled. 'It's been my pleasure.' And it had. She'd lived a few days of utter happiness and it had provided her with memories that would definitely be keeping her warm on the cold English winter nights.

When she finished work, pleased it was a day shift, she headed home, eager to relax and put her feet up. At least, she told herself she was eager. She wasn't scheduled to see Harrison or Yolanda that day, Harrison not needing her babysitting services, and that thought was highly depressing. She liked seeing them, *both* of them, but not that night. Besides, it was almost Yolanda's bedtime.

After she'd had a quick shower and changed into a hot pink tracksuit, all nice and snuggly, there was a knock at her door. When she opened it, she was astonished to see Harrison and Yolanda there.

'We got dinner,' Yolanda announced, as she marched into Amelia's apartment, quite at home.

'We thought it was the least we could do to say thank you,' Harrison said after she'd invited them in. He'd had an overwhelming urge to see her and now that he looked at her, in that bright tracksuit, he was extremely glad he'd given in.

'Ooh. Is pi-i-in-n-nk.' Yolanda ran her hands up and down Amelia's arms and Harrison couldn't believe how jealous he felt of his daughter, being able to touch Amelia when she wanted to.

'I thought you'd like it.' Amelia smiled. 'So, do we need to eat this while it's hot? I'll get some plates. Yolanda, can you help me to set the table, please?'

Yolanda followed Amelia around and Harrison simply watched the two of them. With Yolanda wearing pink and white pyjamas, they were almost like two peas in a pod…just different sizes, of course.

Once more he kept the conversation light, prompting a tired Yolanda to tell Amelia what they'd made.

'A big pickshure for Mrs D.' She stretched her arms out wide.

'A welcome-home poster,' Harrison added. 'And it kept us busy for a good portion of the day.'

'I can well believe it.'

They exchanged hospital news and when Yolanda had yawned twice, Amelia told Harrison to take her home. Reluctantly, he picked his daughter up, the child resting her head on his shoulder. He didn't want to go. He wanted to stay, to prolong the time he had to spend with Amelia. Yes, Mrs D. was coming back tomorrow and he was looking forward to that, but it also meant that Amelia's help would be scaled back and he wouldn't see her nearly as much.

'Listen,' he said when she was about to open the door. 'What are you doing on Saturday morning?'

'Easter Saturday?'

'Yes.'

'Uh…no plans, really. Why?'

'Feel like coming out for breakfast?'

'Breakfast?'

'Sure. Mrs D. and Yolanda will be there.' He smiled down at her. 'I assure you, you'll be quite safe.'

'Are you going out somewhere?'

'We're having breakfast on the beach. It's sort of a tradition. So all you'll need to do is walk outside your door, down the footpath and cross the street and there we'll be, waiting with breakfast on the sand.' He pointed in the direction of the beach. 'A bowl of cereal for me and one for you.'

'Really? Cereal. Be still, my beating heart.'

Harrison chuckled. 'Actually, I think we can do better than just cereal, although if that's all you want, you're more than welcome to eat it.'

'Why on the beach?' She'd never thought of it before but why not? The beach was right there, right outside their windows, so why not make use of it?

'I don't know. We did it for Yolanda's first Easter and we've just sort of continued. We'll have healthy start-the-day-right foods, so hopefully Yolanda will eat more than a bowl of porridge.'

'Oh, well, so long as it's with start-the-day-right foods, you can't possibly go wrong.'

'Funny, AJ.' He shifted Yolanda, who appeared to have fallen asleep. 'You'll come?'

'Will there be any Easter eggs?'

'I thought you didn't like chocolate.'

'I never said I didn't like it. I simply said I prefer savoury to sweet.'

'Well, to answer your question, no. No eggs tomorrow. They're for Sunday. The eggs signify new life, remember. No. No eggs tomorrow.'

'You don't need to convince me,' Amelia said, laughing.

'Good. I'll see you at eight-thirty on Saturday, then.'

'Do I need to bring anything?'

'Just yourself…oh, and your swimmers. We might take a dip before we eat.'

'OK.'

'Sleep sweet, Amelia-Jane.' With that, he opened the door and left, carrying his sleeping daughter home. He carefully put her into her pink and white bed, knowing she'd only stay there for a few hours before joining him in his big king-sized bed because she couldn't sleep. He made himself a drink then sat at the kitchen bench and thought about Amelia. She didn't like fresh flowers and he couldn't give her chocolates but he desperately wanted to give her something. He told himself it would be a thank-you gift for everything she'd done for him and Yolanda that week but he shook his head, knowing he needed to be honest, at least with himself. He wanted to get her something personal, something she could take back to England and remember him by.

So what did a man give a...*friend* for Easter?

On Good Friday, the A and E staff were usually run off their feet and this year was no exception. Amelia had dealt with three drunks, two teenagers who had gone overboard with the happy pills and needed to have their stomachs pumped, one woman with a broken arm after she'd 'fallen' down a flight of stairs and a young man who'd been having heart palpitations. A basic, average late shift.

She'd had conversations with her colleagues, spoken to social workers, contacted parents, checked X-rays and filled in mounds of paperwork, yet the entire time thoughts of Harrison remained at the back of her mind.

Saturday morning dawned bright and early and Amelia worked at containing her excitement at seeing him, having missed him terribly yesterday. She knew she shouldn't. She knew if one day went by when she didn't see her boss that it shouldn't be a big deal, but after spending so much time with them over the past few days, she couldn't help it. How was she ever going to withdraw herself from his life? From Yolanda's?

She shook her head, preferring not to think about it. She closed her apartment door and walked outside, surprised to find so many cars parked and people on the beach at that hour of the morning.

As she walked down the street, she saw Mrs Deveraux come out the house, carrying a large bowl and trying to juggle her walking cane. Amelia called out and Mrs D. turned and smiled as she walked up.

'Let me take that for you,' Amelia said, relieving Mrs D. of her burden.

'Thank you, dear. It's good to see you again.'

'Likewise. How are you feeling? Not overdoing it, I hope.'

'Harrison won't let me.' She pointed across the road. 'He's already over there with Yolanda.' Amelia turned and from where she stood she could see Harrison running down the beach, chasing after his daughter. 'He thought she should get some exercise first. Hopefully, that will help her build up an appetite,' Mrs D. continued.

Amelia nodded and they slowly headed across the road and over the sand dunes to where the beach became flatter. To her surprise, a small table had been set up, with chairs around it and a beach umbrella to provide shade—although it wouldn't provide much at that hour of the morning but, still, it was very picturesque. She put the large bowl of fruit salad down and turned to watch Harrison.

He was wearing knee-length swimming shorts and nothing more. His torso was firm and brown, his legs long and lithe as he pretended to miss capturing his little girl. His hair was ruffled in the breeze and the smile on his face completed the picture of one hundred per cent eye-candy. Amelia found it difficult not to sigh with longing.

Harrison spotted her, waved and then scooped up Yolanda who squealed with delight and giggled with glee, before heading in her direction. 'Hey, AJ. Glad you could come.' He lifted his daughter and blew a raspberry on her tummy before putting her down. She ran off the instant her little feet touched the sand.

Now that he was so close to her...and so much of him was on offer for her to ogle, Amelia found it difficult to know where to look. So she met his gaze and held it, feeling slightly overdressed in her flowing summer skirt and top. She also felt highly self-conscious knowing Mrs D. was taking in every glance, every word and every unspoken word between them.

Harrison reached down and took her hand in his, giving it a little squeeze. 'I really am glad you decided to come.'

Amelia smiled, looked down at their hands, then back to his eyes. 'Me, too.'

'Daddy!' Yolanda called laughingly. 'You tarn't tatch me.'

Harrison reluctantly let go of her hand and shrugged. 'Duty calls,' he said as he took a few steps away. 'Sit down. Be comfortable.' With that, he turned and went to chase his daughter once more. Amelia sat and watched him, laughing at the two of them together. He'd intrigued her right from the first instant she'd met him and now her intrigue had turned to admiration at the way he loved his daughter. It was enough to melt any woman's heart and hers was no exception.

Finally, they were ready to eat and they all enjoyed a feast of cereal, toast, yoghurt, fruit salad, croissants and breakfast muffins. Yolanda did indeed eat quite a bit and her father was very satisfied. It was a picture-perfect morning and Amelia couldn't remember spending a better time at the beach—ever.

Afterwards, Yolanda picked up her bucket and spade and sat down to make sandcastles. 'Daddy,' she called. 'Tum and help me.'

'What's up?' Harrison asked, crossing to his daughter's side.

Yolanda stood there and looked down at the sandcastle she'd made. Her hands were on her hips and she was studying it carefully. 'It need be bigger, Daddy. Much, much bigger.' Now she waved her arms around above her head, showing him how big it needed to be.

'We might need some more help.' Harrison pointed to Amelia.

'Yes.' Yolanda decided her father was right and crossed to Amelia's side, taking her hand. 'Use dis one,' she instructed, putting a sandy bucket onto Amelia's lap. Then she stopped, took a moment to rub her wet and sandy hand over the fabric. 'Dis prwetty.'

'Thank you.' Amelia allowed herself to be pulled up, catching the bucket with her free hand. Next, she found herself sitting on the sand, filling buckets and tipping them over to create the great palace Yolanda was demanding.

'How about getting some shells to decorate it?' she suggested, and Yolanda instantly agreed, tugging Amelia to her feet.

Harrison simply sat there and watched the two of them walk away, hand in hand, their eyes glued to the sand as they looked for pretty shells. Contentment washed over him and tension seeped out as he realised he trusted Amelia. He completely, utterly and totally trusted her with his precious daughter! After Inga he'd thought he'd never trust again yet somehow, during his short acquaintance with Amelia-Jane, his ability to trust had been restored.

By the time Amelia and Yolanda returned from collecting their shells, Harrison had packed everything away. The sandcastle took on an amazing form, with Amelia sculpting the most beautiful structure from sand and water.

'More water, Daddy,' Yolanda said again, holding out a bucket to him.

'Manners,' Harrison reminded her.

'Peeze, Daddy.'

'That's better.' Harrison met Amelia's gaze as he took the bucket from his daughter and headed off. She watched him, admiring the magnificence of his body. Thankfully, before they'd settled down to eat, he'd donned an old T-shirt which had the words 'Professional Beach Bum' written on it. Amelia totally believed it because he certainly looked the part.

Hats, sunglasses and the constant slathering on of sunscreen were all part of the Aussie beach code of practice but when she'd watched Harrison rub cream into his arms, legs and face earlier, she'd been mesmerised…much as she was now.

She continued to watch him as he scooped up some water, navigating his way through the throng of people and little kids enjoying the shallows, the lifeguards on duty making sure people swam in the safety zone between the flags.

When he returned, he sat down next to his daughter, who was all but lying on Amelia's legs as they patted and shaped the sand. Because Yolanda was close, it now meant Harrison was equally as close, his leg brushing one of hers causing a powerful jolt of desire to explode within her. Their eyes met and held, both of them too stunned at their mutual need to hide their reactions.

'Need more shells,' Yolanda said, and scrambled to her feet. 'Tum on, Meel-ya.' She reached for Amelia's hand but Harrison protested on her behalf.

'Why don't you let Amelia have a rest this time? Besides, the shells you find are always the prettiest because *you* are the prettiest.'

Yolanda nodded as though his words made complete sense. She started off but Harrison told her to just look in the area they were sitting in. The number of beach-goers had almost doubled since they'd first started their breakfast and it would be all too easy to lose sight of her.

'So…' he drawled as he patted the sand. 'This is quite a castle. In fact, it's a brilliant sculpture.'

'Yolanda's very clever. She knows exactly what she wants.'

'And you're able to shape and mould and give it to her. This isn't just a sandcastle, AJ, it's a work of art.'

Amelia smiled and shrugged. 'I used to sculpt when I was younger and, besides, the sand here is so fine and easy to use.'

'You don't sculpt any more?'

'No time.'

'Come on. Tell the truth. I know how busy your job is, remember. I've been there, I've done it and, despite what people think, doctors do get a few hours off here and there.'

Amelia dipped her hands in the bucket of water and smoothed a section of the turrets with her fingers. 'I stopped and until today I haven't had the urge to start again.'

'Why did you stop?'

'I uh…got sick. Kind of.'

Harrison sat up straight. 'Are you OK now?' His tone was filled with concern. 'Is everything all right?'

Amelia was touched. 'It was quite a number of years ago and yes, I'm…fine.'

'Do you think you can tell me what happened?' Harrison glanced at her and then back to where Yolanda was starting to wander a bit further away. 'Hold that thought,' he said, and ran off to collect his daughter. When they returned, both adults allowed themselves to be distracted by Yolanda until she declared the masterpiece was finished. Mrs D., who had been watching them from the shade of her umbrella, pulled out a camera and took some photographs of the prettiest princess palace ever.

'That's simply amazing,' she said as she took a snap from a different angle. 'You're extremely talented, Amelia.'

Amelia merely smiled and stood, brushing the sand from her clothes. Harrison watched her, mesmerised by the way she fluffed her fingers through her short hair, her skirt blowing gently around her legs with the slight sea breeze.

'Why don't you two go for a walk?' Mrs D. suggested quietly. 'It's time for Yolanda to be inside, enjoying the air-conditioning, and I could certainly do with resting my leg.'

'OK.' Harrison wasn't about to look a gift horse in the mouth. Time alone with Amelia-Jane…just what he wanted. Harrison told his daughter he was going to go for a walk with Amelia, and Yolanda was more than happy to let him go, especially when Mrs D. was offering icy-poles and a video of Yolanda's favourite kids' entertainment group.

'What parent can compete with four grown men, wearing colourful skivvies, singing and dancing their way into our children's hearts?' he said as they waved to Yolanda before starting off down the beach. As they navigated their way around a few people sunbathing, Amelia wondered if he was going to hold her hand. She hoped so.

Her question was answered a moment later when

she stumbled over the undulating sand and he instantly reached out to steady her. When she was steady, he didn't let go, linking their fingers, the warmth from his arm running up hers. She wasn't sure whether to say something about it or simply to let it happen.

'It's all right if I hold your hand, isn't it?' he asked, then a smile touched his lips.

Amelia nodded. 'It's just been a long time since anyone's held my hand in this way.'

'That's kinda sad, Amelia-Jane.'

'Probably,' she sighed.

They walked in silence, going further down the beach where it was slightly less crowded so they didn't need to dodge as many people. 'I meant to tell you, your file finally arrived from Brisbane.'

'Oh, good.'

'I find it interesting that you've broken your year in Australia into four three-month rotations. That's not normal.'

Amelia shrugged. 'I wanted to see as much of Australia as I could.'

'So you've seen Perth, Melbourne, Brisbane and now Adelaide. Right?'

'Yes.'

'Three months hardly gives you time to make a lot of friends, AJ.' He felt her tense at his words and realised he'd struck a nerve. She loosened her grip on his fingers but he didn't release her hand.

'I'm not looking for friends, Harrison. I'm looking to finish my training.'

'Your file doesn't say anything about you being sick.'

'It won't affect my job performance, if that's what

you're worried about.' She hadn't meant to snap but her words came out brisk.

'That's not what I'm worried about and you know it,' he countered. 'Why did you stop sculpting? Why were you sick? Are you better now?' He shook his head. 'I don't mean to bombard you but there's so much I don't know and I want to, AJ. I want to know about you very much.'

'What's the point, Harrison? I'll be gone soon.'

'The point? The point is, I like you.'

'Oh.' She didn't know how to respond to that and the annoyance she'd felt at him quizzing her disappeared. In its place came a feeling so warm and encompassing she wanted it to last for ever. No man had ever affected her the way Harrison did.

'Please, AJ. Talk to me. It's all right.' He stopped walking and turned her to face him. Gently, he lifted her sunglasses and placed them on top of her head, before lifting his own. 'I understand it's difficult but if there's going to be anything between us, AJ, I need to know.'

'Anything but friendship?'

'I think we know friendship is only a part of what we feel for each other. I'm not denying its importance—in fact, after one failed relationship, I've come to realise a bonding of the minds is more important than a bonding of bodies.' He took both her hands in his. 'But a friendship, one where we can grow, needs to be forged with open and honest communication.'

The way Harrison was talking made Amelia want to run a mile. She couldn't get involved with him, they both knew that but she also knew what he said was true. They *did* feel more than friendship for each other but was it wise to take it any further?

She found it difficult to look at him, wanting to

believe in what had been building between them during the past few weeks but also knowing she'd be setting herself up for an even bigger hurt later on. 'I agree,' she finally said. 'But…'

'But?' he prompted.

'I'm leaving at the end of June. I don't think it's wise to get any closer than we are already.'

'What if it's too late for that?'

Again, his words stunned her and she started to tremble. 'Is it?'

'I like you, AJ. Is it so wrong that I want to know more about you? Can't you bring yourself to trust me enough to at least tell me why you were sick?'

Amelia sighed and closed her eyes for a moment, wondering if she was making a mountain out of a molehill. She wasn't sure but while she didn't like blurting out her past to all and sundry, she also recognised Harrison meant more to her than just a passing acquaintance. She opened her eyes and met his gaze.

'I have endometriosis.'

Harrison paused, almost waiting for more. When it didn't come, he nodded slowly. 'That's why you were sick? Why you stopped sculpting?' He knew there were varying degrees of endometriosis but if she'd been sick, it probably meant her case had been extreme.

'Yes.' Amelia dropped his hands and sat down on the sand, staring out to sea.

'Is it hereditary?'

She nodded. 'I'm an only child, my parents were in their forties when they had me. My mother suffered badly from endometriosis and back in those days all the doctors thought women exaggerated their pain whenever menstruating. Mum was bad, though, and finally was able to find a doctor who would listen. After twenty childless years of marriage and many operations she somehow became pregnant with me. She was bedridden for the entire pregnancy and even then I was premature.' She pulled her knees to her chest and hugged them.

Harrison continued to wait.

'I've been on medication for it since I was a teenager and while it's under control I still get days when I get depressed and upset. Lethargy and headaches sometimes strike but eating right and ensuring I don't exhaust myself are key elements in controlling them as well. When I was eighteen, I had a conservative laparotomy.' Amelia couldn't look at him while she spoke.

'They were initially just going to burn the cysts off, remove the adhesions and endometrial implants, but when they opened me up it was far worse than they'd originally thought. I woke up to discover my body was minus one ovary and Fallopian tube. Of course, I knew the risks involved and had discussed this possibility with my surgeon, but to have it actually happen…'

'AJ.' The emotion in his voice was what brought her tears to the surface and when he gathered her close, she went without hesitation. Neither of them spoke for five minutes, Amelia listening to the beat of his heart and comforted at the feeling of having someone hold her.

Eventually, she eased back but took hold of his hand, entwining their fingers tightly as though she never wanted to let go.

'So the chances of you having children?' he asked, and Amelia closed her eyes. She'd told him enough for one day. Dredging up the emotions was never easy and she'd had enough. She was drained. He was waiting for an answer, though, and she opened her eyes, looking out at the surfers, so wild and carefree—at least, that's how they appeared. Her answer was to shrug and Harrison nodded, accepting that.

'This is why you find it difficult being around small children? Babies?'

'They're always so gorgeous, Yolanda especially. She may have her problems and you may have some humdingers just waiting to happen but, Harrison, at least you appreciate her. You love her so much and it's evident every time you're together.'

'She's my world,' he said easily.

'Exactly. Children are so precious, so valuable. People who become parents should know how lucky they are—there are so many out there who might never get that chance.'

Harrison nodded, in total agreement with her, and they were both quiet for a while, both looking out to sea and both lost in their thoughts. Now that she'd told him, he'd probably leave her alone and that thought made her sad. There was only one other man she'd told, one very important man she'd confided in because they'd been heading to a serious place in their relationship. It had happened a few years after her operation and where she'd thought he'd loved her enough to take her as she was, she'd found out she'd been wrong. The news hadn't been what he'd wanted to hear and although he assured her he was fine, he'd high-tailed it out of her life as fast as possible. That had been over ten years ago now and Amelia had grown wiser.

'Thank you for talking to me,' he finally said.

'I'll confess, it wasn't easy.'

'You're not used to opening up to people, are you Amelia-Jane?' he said gently.

'No. Not about that.'

'This is a step in the right direction,' he said firmly.

'It is?'

'Yes. We've both opened up and that's a good thing.'

'I guess.'

He smiled at her. 'You guess? It's good because it means we're ready for the next step.'

'Step? What step?' she asked.

'The steps of getting to know each other.' His lips were curved into a small smile which slowly disappeared as he carefully lifted her hat and sunglasses off her head and then tenderly brushed his fingers through her hair, loving the colour. 'You're beautiful, Amelia-Jane.' His voice was soft, intimate and she couldn't believe how incredible he made her feel with his lovely words. He brought his fingers across her cheek then tilted her chin up so their lips could meet.

It was tentative at first, both of them wanting it, still not sure of the other, and his touch was feather-light. Once, twice his lips brushed across hers and she found herself trembling with repressed desire. The next time he touched her, she leaned in closer, adding more pressure to let him know she wanted this as much as he did. Need and desire ripped through him like nothing he'd ever felt before. Who was this woman who could make his blood boil with such ease? He felt like an out-of-control adolescent, unable to contain the way she made him feel. He tried to remember if he'd ever felt this way before but his mind came up blank. She surrounded him, not only by her scent but by her total ca-

pitulation, and he enjoyed every single part of it. The
giving, the receiving.

He drew her closer, needing to feel her body pressed
close to his but not wanting to rush her. Impatience and
patience warred within him but it seemed she was also
fighting a losing battle as she once more increased the
pressure of the kiss. She leaned in, opened her mouth
more, drew his lower lip between hers and nibbled at it
with her teeth. There was no way he could resist what
she was offering, her sweetness encompassing him as
he took what she was so willing to give, pleased that
when a ripple of excitement coursed through her, he
affected her just as much as she affected him.

When he finally touched his tongue to hers, she
thought she might burst with wanting. He was driving
her wild, taking her places she'd never been before.
Usually when it came to experiencing something new,
she would shy away until she'd had a chance to figure
out all the angles. Yet this time she didn't care. He made
her feel so wonderful, so cherished and feminine,
simply by the way he was holding her, by the way he
was kissing her, by the way he seemed more than happy
to lose himself completely in her.

She raised her hands and touched his chest and when
she made that initial contact he strained a little before
leaning into the touch. When her palms were pressed
against his chest, her fingers exploring the contours of
the firm torso she'd been itching to touch since she'd first
arrived that morning, he groaned with crazed delight.

It was maddening. Totally maddening what was happening between them. The pheromones whirled around
them, enticing them to take it to the next level, and
when he nibbled on her lip then ran his tongue along

first the lower then upper lip, Amelia moaned with shivering delight and wrapped her arms about him, her fingers impatiently urging his head down, holding it in place while they gave way to their mounting hunger.

Nothing mattered. Nothing at all. It was just the two of them. The need. The desire. The passion that continued to flare. The past, the future were forgotten. There was only the present, only this moment in which they both seemed content to live for ever, even though both acknowledged it was impossible.

Eventually the need for oxygen broke them apart but Harrison merely used it as an excuse to press butterfly kisses across her cheek and round to her ear where he nuzzled, his breath coming out in gasps as they slowly floated back to earth.

'Wow.' Amelia panted the word into his shoulder, her eyes closed as she revelled in the way she was allowed to touch him, her fingers running lightly up and down his back in a sweet caress.

'You can say that again.'

'Wow.'

He chuckled and reluctantly eased back to rest his forehead against hers. 'Amelia-Jane. You are a special woman. Did you know that?'

'Uh…'

His smile increased. 'You find it difficult to accept compliments.' She merely shrugged. 'Believe me when I say I find you irresistible.'

'I want to believe it but…'

'But?'

'But if I do, it means I'm opening myself up.'

'That's definitely the hard part and I'm sorry if you feel things got out of control just now.' He lifted his head and looked around them, realising they were getting a few strange looks from people. 'Although, thankfully, not *too* out of control.' He gathered her to him, pressing a kiss to the top of her head. 'You make me forget where I am, AJ.'

'That's how I feel.'

A loud cry pierced the air, snapping them out of their bubble. A young swimmer was hurtling out of the waves, running as fast as he could towards the lifeguard. 'Shark!' The teenager screamed. 'Shark! There's a shark out there. It's got someone!'

CHAPTER SEVEN

HARRISON felt Amelia stiffen in his arms and when he looked at her, she'd gone deathly pale. 'AJ?'

No response. He gave her a little shake. 'Amelia?'

She snapped her head around and looked at him, her eyes wide with fear, her body beginning to tremble. Panic gripped her and breathing became erratic.

'What's wrong?'

'I hate sharks.' She swallowed. 'I'm English. Shark attacks aren't exactly common at home.'

'You'll be fine,' he said pulling her to her feet and peering out to sea. 'Same as any triage. One step at a time.'

Amelia glanced around. She could hear the screams of the people, could smell the fear in the air, and she swallowed the distasteful realisation she was about to become a part of this situation. It was their job and they were on hand. Both of them, trained A and E doctors at the right place at the right time, could go along way to saving the surfer's life.

'AJ, there'll be blood and lacerations. Amputations are common with shark attack as well.' Harrison grabbed her hand and started walking as he spoke, Amelia following alongside him. 'You've dealt with those types of injuries before. You'll be fine.'

The lifeguard was peering through his binoculars to where the teenager who'd raised the alarm was pointing. A team of lifesavers was coming from the clubhouse with their emergency boat. People were everywhere, streaming out of the water, gathering up toddlers and babies. One woman was calling her daughter's name as she searched frantically for the child. Harrison silently thanked Mrs D. for taking Yolanda back to the house. At least he knew she was safe.

The lifeguard on duty was being bombarded with people and questions and was trying to keep a state of calm on the beach. Many people started packing up and heading for their cars. Others lined the water's edge and looked out to where there were several surfers, all heading over to help whoever was in trouble. They stuck together and adhered to the rule—never surf alone.

'Let's go offer our services,' he said, and she nodded, her gaze still scanning the waves out to sea, trying to make out what was happening. Harrison looked as well. The surfers were starting to head to shore, the lifeguard rescue boat only just hitting the water. 'Those first few minutes are going to be critical.'

'What do you want me to do?' she asked, her voice calm, her breathing even.

'Go to my house and ask Mrs D. for my medical kit. She knows where it is.'

'Do I need to call the ambulance?'

'I'm sure that's already been done.' Harrison turned and headed over to the lifeguards, who were setting up an area to accept the surfer. His mates almost had him out of the water, the patient being balanced on the boards of others.

Harrison went up to the lifeguard in charge and in-

troduced himself. 'I'm a doctor,' he said, and the relief
that came over the young man's face would have been
almost comical if the situation hadn't been so dire.

'Great. Great. I'm Jonah, by the way. Uh…we're
gonna put him here.' He indicated the area to his left,
which had a medical kit and a pile of blankets.

'Good. Get these people back. I'm going to need
some room.'

Jonah turned to one of his colleagues and yelled in-
structions.

'I'm presuming the ambulance has been called?'
Harrison asked.

'Yes.'

'My colleague is just over the road at my house,
getting my medical bag.' Harrison bent down and
opened the first-aid kit to check what it held. 'When she
arrives, she'll need to be let through without question.
She'll be carrying a black medical bag so I think you'll
recognise her.'

'So…uh…you know what to expect, then?' Jonah
asked.

'If you're interested in my credentials, I'm the
director of Accident and Emergency at Glenelg General.
Can't get more qualified than that.' Harrison glanced up
the beach and saw AJ making her way across the sand.
When he looked the other way at the water, the surfers,
with the assistance of the lifeguards, were carrying the
injured man towards them.

'Get back. Make room,' Jonah was ordering.

People were such sticky-beaks at times, Harrison
thought, wishing they'd all go, but he focused his
thoughts on what was going to happen next.

Amelia arrived about ten seconds before the surfer

was carried over and she instantly opened Harrison's medical bag and began checking the contents. 'You have saline—good.'

'Is Yolanda OK?' he asked.

'She's watching TV,' Amelia answered.

'Good.'

When the surfer was placed before them, Amelia frowned for a moment. The man was alive and conscious. For some strange reason she'd thought he'd be either half-mangled or almost dead. Instead, he was chatting away as though being attacked by a shark happened to him every day. These Aussies! She doubted she'd ever understand them.

'What's your name?' Harrison asked as he reached for the scissors and began slicing open the surfer's wetsuit.

'Troy.'

'How old are you, Troy?'

'Twenty.'

'Been surfing long?'

'Ten years.'

'Allergic to anything?'

'Nope.'

'Good.' While he'd been talking, Harrison had done a quick appraisal of the injuries, as had Amelia. There was a lot of blood around the foot of the right leg and she ripped a sterile pad from its wrapper and applied pressure over the area with the most blood. As she held it firmly, she could feel something was missing and when she lifted the pad a moment later she realised Troy was missing his forth and fifth toes.

'Can you take a deep breath for me?' Harrison asked, and was pleased with Troy's effort. 'Lacerations to right arm and right leg,' he said quietly yet firmly, and Amelia knew he was talking directly to her. Harrison felt Troy's head. 'Got any bumps up here?'

'No.'

He held up his finger. 'Look at this.' He moved his finger from side to side and up and down before asking for his medical torch. Amelia pulled it from the bag and handed it to him.

'Amputation of forth and fifth metatarsals. Increased blood loss.'

Harrison nodded and called one of the lifeguards over. 'Get a blanket on him. We need to keep his body warm. Find something to elevate his leg with.' As he spoke, he pulled a few padded bandages from the medical kit and pressed them on the injured area. 'Jonah,' he called. 'Hold this.'

'Is he gonna be all right?' Troy's mate asked.

'He's going to do just fine,' Harrison answered, not looking up at him but performing neurovascular obser-vations again. He checked Troy's pupils. 'Equal and reacting,' he announced. 'Pulse is starting to weaken. Troy. Take another deep breath in for me.' He kept his fingers pressed to Troy's wrist. 'And again. That's it.' He nodded. 'Better. Keep that breathing up. Not too fast. We don't need you getting dizzy.' Harrison now looked at Troy's friend. 'Make sure he keeps those deep breaths up.' The other young man was pale as well, but hope-fully because Harrison had given him something to do, he would calm down. They didn't need him or anyone else going into shock.

'AJ?'

'Bleeding controlled,' she said as she bandaged up Troy's foot. 'I'll get a drip set up next.'

'Good.' Harrison took a closer look at the lacerations to the arm and thigh. 'He tried to take a good chunk out of your leg, mate.'

'Yeah.'

'In fact, it looks as though he just missed your femoral artery.'

'That good?'

'That's brilliant, mate.' Harrison checked Troy's pulse. 'Keep that deep breathing up. We like our patients breathing, don't we, AJ?'

'Absolutely.' She clipped the tubes together and attached them to the bag of saline. 'Here.' She handed the bag to the lifeguard who'd helped her elevate Troy's leg on an Esky. 'Hold this.' She withdrew the needle and shifted over to Troy's left side, rubbing an alcohol wipe on his arm. 'Not squeamish with needles, Troy?' She knew that he probably wouldn't even be aware of it going in because of everything else his body was trying to cope with, but if he looked at it, she didn't want him passing out.

'Nah. I'm fine.'

'Good.' She inserted the needle into his arm but a second later there was a thud next to them as Troy's friend keeled over.

'Check him,' Harrison ordered Jonah.

'Just fainted,' came the report, and a moment later Troy's friend came round, more embarrassed then anything else.

'Hey,' Troy said to Jonah. 'Do you have to report this?'

'Of course we do. A shark attack is very serious.'

'But the shark. They'll kill it.'

'That's what happens when one attacks. Its destruction is ordered and that's all there is to it,' Jonah said with authority in his voice. 'We can't risk them attacking someone else.'

'But I'm fine and Great Whites are a protected species.'

'It could have killed you,' Jonah pointed out.

Amelia was surprised at Troy's attitude. She'd never thought she'd hear a person who'd just been attacked by a shark advocating for them. She was stunned.

'But surely you don't need to report it,' Troy said.

'It's my job to—'

'Enough!' Harrison said, glancing at both men and then AJ. 'Now is not the time for bickering or this type of discussion. When is the ambulance due? Someone find out.' He looked at Amelia again. 'You OK?'

'Fine.'

'Good.' He returned his attention to Troy's lacerations. 'These will need suturing,' he said, finishing off the pressure bandage. 'AJ, obs, please.'

Amelia reached for the medical torch and checked Troy's eyes, then his pulse, which was still a little weak. 'Deep breaths, Troy.' His face had a little more colour in it and his lips and fingernails were turning from their earlier bluish tinge to more of a healthy pink. 'Any dizziness? Nausea?' she asked, her fingers still pressed to his pulse.

'No.'

'Ambulance has just arrived,' someone called, and the crowd around them parted as the paramedics carried their stretcher and equipment down the beach.

'Amelia?' Gina Douglas, the first paramedic, said, and then looked at Harrison. 'Hey, Harrison.'

'Hi, Gina, Ben,' said Harrison, nodding at the second paramedic. 'Good to see you.' Gina and Ben knelt down and started hooking the oxy-viva up, placing the non-rebreather mask over Troy's mouth and nose.

'Twenty-year-old male.' Harrison started the report.

'Multiple lacerations to the right arm and right leg. Spontaneous amputation of the fourth and fifth metatarsals. No head trauma, pupils equal and reacting to light. Pulse slightly weak and rapid at times. Saline given and no analgesics as yet.'

'What do you want to give him?' Gina asked as she adjusted the oxygen levels.

'Troy, are you allergic to morphine?' Harrison said.

'No. I've had it before and I was fine with it.'

'What did you have it for?' Harrison asked.

'Uh…after having my appendix out when I was seventeen.'

'Are you currently on any medication?' Amelia asked as she adjusted the blanket around Troy and saw the appendicectomy scar.

'No. Uh…I was drinking last night.'

'You should be fine,' Harrison said, and when Gina had drawn up the injection Harrison administered it. They managed to lift Troy onto the stretcher using the pat-slide and soon he was being carried up to the waiting ambulance. Jonah, the lifeguard, who'd taken over holding the saline drip bag, walked beside him.

Amelia glanced at Harrison as they gathered up his medical supplies and followed the patient up to the ambulance.

'Are you all right?' Harrison asked, taking her hand in his as they walked across the sand.

'Sure. It was just like you said. Take it one step at a time and follow the rules of triage.'

Harrison smiled and tugged her closer, putting his arm around her shoulders and dropping a kiss to the top of her head. They were almost at the kerb now and Gina climbed out of the back doors of the ambulance. As she shut them, she glanced at the two doctors and smiled. Amelia shifted slightly, feeling a little uncomfortable, but Harrison didn't drop his arm.

'Thanks, Gina,' Amelia said. 'I can do any paperwork on this when I come in this afternoon.'

'Sure. I'll leave it in your pigeonhole.' With that, the dark-haired paramedic went around to the driver's side and with a flash of lights and the whirring of the siren, the ambulance drove off.

Harrison turned and slipped his arms about Amelia's waist and she didn't hesitate to go into them. It felt nice, to be held close by Harrison, nice and re-assuring. She couldn't remember ever feeling as comfortable with a man as she did with him. She closed her eyes and breathed in deeply, the salt and sand mixed with his own personal scent a memory she would keep for ever.

The wind blew around them, the temperature dropping momentarily as the sun was hidden behind a cloud, and Amelia shivered, the action causing Harrison to tighten his hold on her. Was that where she was deep down inside? Was she behind a cloud, trying to figure out how to get out, to find the sun again? She listened to his heartbeat, so loud, so strong and so powerful.

'You feel so right, AJ,' he murmured, and she leaned back, looking deeply into his brown eyes. 'I can't explain it but it's just the way it feels.'

Amelia nodded and sighed.

'Come on, you need to rest if you're working this afternoon.' He shifted so they could walk, one arm still about her shoulders, holding her close. Now that he'd touched her, kissed her, he felt an overwhelming need to protect her and he didn't take his duties lightly.

She pointed to his house. 'I might just go and say goodbye to Yolanda, if that's all right.'

'Sure. Of course.'

Yolanda was up and dancing to her favourite DVD, but when she saw Amelia she broke off and came running over, holding her chubby arms out.

'Meel-ya. Tum and dance.'

'Can I watch you dance?' Amelia asked, and found a willing participant in the three-year-old. 'You are such a beautiful dancer,' she praised as the girl wove and wiggled around the room in time to the music, copying the actions of the actors on television. She ended up staying for three songs but finally was able to say goodbye, Yolanda dismissing her with an uninterested wave of her hand.

'I'm just going to walk Amelia home,' Harrison called to Mrs D., who was sitting at the bench, resting her leg, while she read a book.

'All right, dear.'

They walked down the footpath, Harrison linking their hands. Amelia was simply amazing. This woman who had been through so much. This woman who had opened up to him. This woman who fitted perfectly in his arms, against his body, their lips pressed together.

It was as though they'd travelled so far through their lives, experiencing disappointment, turmoil, pain and grief to arrive here and now. Harrison had always thought that one day he might meet someone new, someone he could learn to trust. They'd become friends, their relationship would grow and he'd eventually marry once more, giving Yolanda a mother who loved her as well as siblings to play with.

'Have you ever told any other man about your operation? About what you live with every day?' As a doctor, he'd treated women and young girls who'd been afflicted with the condition and from what he'd read and studied, endometriosis was a very painful disease to have.

'Once. A long time ago.'

'Let me guess. You told him about your operation and he bolted?'

'Exactly.'

'Which makes trusting difficult.'

'It does.'

'I understand that. Really I do, and I'm honoured you trusted me because it's not an easy thing to give, especially once it's been abused.'

'Your wife?'

'Ex-wife. Well, technically she wasn't but if Inga had lived, we would have divorced. It was the right thing to do, it was what I *needed* to do for both Yolanda and myself.' He looked at their entwined fingers and rubbed his thumb over her knuckle. 'Two weeks after Inga moved out, I received a call from the police, asking me to meet them at the hospital. I had to identify her body.'

'Oh, Harrison.' Amelia gasped, her heart going out to him.

'Her blood-alcohol reading was well over the limit and she had been driving.'

Amelia gaped at him unable to fathom how horrible that would have been.

'It was a difficult time and Yolanda wasn't doing well either.'

'But you got through it. That shows how strong you are deep down inside.' He shrugged and Amelia continued as though she needed to convince him. 'I know how important Yolanda is to you. It's clear to anyone when they see the two of you together. You're a wonderful father and I have no doubt you will raise a daughter who is self-sufficient and self-assured. No parent could ask for more than that.'

He sighed. 'Some days, though, AJ, I wonder what on earth I'm doing. Her therapeutic management, the exercises, the constant need for supervision, it's all so intense. There are days when she simply sits and stares at a wall because she can't cope with the world around her. It all becomes too much. What if she doesn't grow out of that? What if I can't fix her?'

'You don't need to *fix* her, Harrison, and from what I've seen, you're doing an amazing job. You haven't left her in a daycare centre, you have specialised one-on-one care in her own environment provided by a person you both love. You have a demanding job but working in a nine-to-five position is the best place for you to be and you've realised that.' Amelia's tone was imploring, desperate for him to believe every word she was saying.

'Yolanda is wonderful. The fact that she was diagnosed so early is a credit to you. You knew what the situation was, you knew what signs and symptoms to look for and because of that, she has benefited.'

'But you still picked up that there was something wrong with her.'

'Yes, but I'm a doctor so that's different. Besides, it's not as though you're trying to hide Yolanda's disability. You're simply trying to give her what she needs, the tools, if you like, to make the most of her life and to grow into an independent woman.'

'You think so?'

Amelia couldn't believe his self-doubt. He had

always seemed so strong, so in charge. 'Yes, I do. You're a wonderful father, Harrison. Try not to doubt that.'

He was silent for a moment, letting her words sink in. 'You're good for me, Amelia-Jane. Do you realise that? I've really enjoyed spending time with you today and I can't thank you enough for everything you did for Yolanda during the week.'

Amelia was filled with warmth. 'It was my pleasure. She's such a joy to be around.'

'I don't want to impose on you but Mrs D.'s recovery is going to take at least another fortnight before she is back on her feet, so to speak. Would it still be possible for you to call in, to check on how things are going? When you have your days off, of course.'

'Sure. I said I'd be happy to help and I still am.' She just didn't seem to able to say no to this man.

'That really means a lot to me, AJ. I'll see you tonight, then.'

'What?' They were outside her apartment door now and she turned to look at him in total confusion. 'I'm working.'

'I know. You finish around midnight, right?'

'Some time around then, yes.'

'Well, I'll come and walk you home from the hospital. Make sure you're safe.'

'I was going to take a taxi.'

'It's forecast to be a lovely evening.'

'Harrison, I don't understand.'

'You said you'd be willing to help when you weren't working.'

'And I am.'

'Well, you won't be working then.'

'And you'll need help?'

'I'll need help walking you home. How can I do that if you're not there?'

Amelia closed her eyes for a second and shook her head. 'You're confusing me.'

Harrison raised his eyebrows, his lips twitching into a grin. 'Good.' He leaned down and gave her a peck on the lips before turning and walking away.

Amelia pulled her keys from her skirt pocket and unlocked her door, her body still getting over the feel of the brief kiss he'd given her. The man was crazy. Why did he want to walk her home at midnight? She wasn't even sure she should have agreed to help him over the next few weeks. Yes, the last few days had been amazing but she could feel herself getting in way over her head and she had to pull back…but she didn't want to.

She groaned as she walked into her apartment. 'I'm so confused.'

CHAPTER EIGHT

WHEN Amelia arrived at work that afternoon, she'd pushed her confusion to the back of her mind and was ready to focus on her job. As she walked through the hospital, she realised she was getting little smiles from people...different smiles from the usual.

When the door to the change rooms opened, she turned and found herself face to face with Tina. 'So? Tell me. The hospital is abuzz with the news that you and Harrison are a couple. As I hardly saw you last week, due to the fact that you were off playing happy families with him, I can't say I'm all that surprised, but anyway...tell me the latest.'

'Well...' Amelia began. 'We've kind of...connected.' She turned and closed her locker door.

'That's a good thing, right?'

'How? How can it be a good thing? I have ten weeks left in this country.'

'But you've just said you connected with him.' Tina paused. 'Ooh. Connected lips?'

Amelia sighed and turned away from Tina.

'You did, didn't you? He kissed you. I can see it. It's written all over your face.'

'It is?' She peered in the mirror.

'I meant figuratively.' Tina laughed. 'Gee, happy families must agree with you.'

'Oh, it does. I don't want it to but I can't help it. I like spending time with him, with Yolanda.'

'Then spend time with him. You *only* have ten weeks.'

'But it's wrong to get involved and then just leave.'

'Is it? Look, how many times has this sort of thing happened to you? Like *never*, Amelia. Harrison—if he makes you feel something, then surely you owe it to yourself to find out what might happen.'

'I have to leave the country.'

'And why should that stop you from exploring this?'

'Because of Yolanda.'

'No. You're just using her as an excuse. You're scared. You're so scared that he'll reject you like that drongo did all those years ago.'

'I cannot have children, Tina. You don't think that would matter to him?'

'How do I know? Ask Harrison.'

'I can't.'

'Why not?'

'Because he'll reject me. It's so obvious he wants more children and why wouldn't he? He's a brilliant father. He deserves to find a woman who can give him what he needs.'

'What if you're that woman? What if you're reject-ing him? Ever thought of that?'

Amelia was silent for a moment as Tina's words sank in. 'No. I haven't thought of it that way.' She sighed. 'I gotta go.'

Amelia focused on her work, seeing her first patient before tracking down Troy who was settled in the orthopaedic ward, still waiting to see an orthopod about his foot.

'Hi, there,' he said when she walked over to his bed. 'Thanks for coming to see me.'

'I'm surprised you don't have more visitors,' Amelia said.

'My parents have just gone to get something to eat. Now that they've seen I'm OK, Mum can start to relax.'

'I'm glad. You were very lucky, Troy.' Her words were soft but Troy merely laughed.

'Luck doesn't have anything to do with it. The shark didn't mean any harm.'

'How can you say that? It might have killed you.'

'But it didn't and I'll tell you why.'

'I'm listening.'

'Because I wasn't surfing alone. I had mates there and they were on that shark, breaking me free before even I knew what was happening. Careful surfers know what to do, know what to expect. We had our anti-shark packs on. We're not stupid but, still, things happen.'

'How can you be so calm about it?'

'The same way you were calm when you were dealing with my injuries. You're a doctor. You're trained to deal with things when the body goes wrong. I'm a surfer—professional beach bum.' The words were said with a smile and Amelia immediately thought of Harrison and his T-shirt. Every thing in her world seemed to come back to him, wherever she was or whatever she was doing.

'Will you ever surf again?'

'Sure.'

Amelia was speechless and stared at him open-mouthed.

'It's in my blood, it's a part of who I am. I guess that seems reckless and careless to you but you wouldn't stop practising medicine if something went wrong with your body. You'd get it fixed and get back to doing what you do best.'

He had a point. That was exactly what she'd done after her own body had failed to co-operate with her plans for the future. 'You've made a valid point, Troy.' She smiled. 'Just concentrate on getting better.'

'Will do.'

She nodded and started to walk away.

'Oh, and, Doc…'

She turned back.

'Thanks…for, uh…you know…fixin' me up.' This time it was Troy who had tears in his eyes and she realised that his lucky escape had affected him far more than he was letting on. She nodded, her smile increasing before she headed back to A and E.

The next few hours ticked by, Tina not saying one more word about Harrison, which Amelia was grateful for. As they seemed unusually quiet for a Saturday evening, she had a lot of time to think…and she didn't want to think.

Amelia's head slumped forward onto the table in the tearoom where she was having her dinner-break. The whole time she'd been thinking about Harrison and trying to figure out what to do next. The man occupied her thoughts constantly and it was getting more and more difficult to shove him to the side when she needed to focus on work. She moaned, not at all sure what she was supposed to do.

'That good, eh?' a deep voice she recognised all too well said, and she sat up straight, eyes wide, and looked at Harrison. 'What…are you doing here?' Her heart leapt in her throat at the sight of him. Slowly, she drank her fill, wondering how he could look equally as handsome in jeans and T-shirt, which he was wearing now, as he did in either a suit or swimming shorts. She'd only seen him that morning yet until he'd stood in the doorway, she hadn't realised how badly she'd missed him. 'Is Yolanda all right?'

'Yes.'

'What are you doing here, then? Mrs D.?'

'Yolanda and Mrs D. are both fine, AJ. Tina called me in.'

'Why?'

'Big emergency.' Harrison came and sat down beside her. 'You don't know?'

'I've been on break for the past half-hour.' She shifted slightly, trying to put a bit of distance between them. Her nose was attuned to his scent and she could feel herself crumbling with need and longing.

He nodded and leaned closer. Amelia automatically leaned back in her chair. 'I won't bite,' he said softly. 'Not unless you want me to.'

'Harrison!' It was a cheesy line at best but it had the full effect. His eyes were so deep, so vibrant that she struggled to ignore how incredible the man was. She swallowed over the sudden dryness in her throat, her gaze flicked down to his lips and her own parted with a burning desperation to have his mouth on hers once more. She looked back at his eyes and realised he knew exactly where her thoughts were.

Harrison leaned back and took a deep breath, holding it then letting it out before he indicated the doorway. 'Shall we go see what Tina has to report?' He held out his hand to her and Amelia looked at it, knowing she should refuse but finding it impossible to pass up another opportunity to touch him. When she slid her hand into his, felt the warmth of his skin on hers, her heart rate, which had only just started to return to normal, picked up instantaneously. Once she was standing, he squeezed her fingers slightly. 'Let's go, Dr Watson.'

He continued to hold her hand as they walked through A and E towards the nurses' station. A few staff saw them together and smiled, one porter even giving Harrison a friendly pat on the back.

'Way to go, boss,' he said, grinning from ear to ear.

'Ah, Amelia,' Tina said. 'I see Harrison found you. Have a nice dinner?'

'Yes, thank you.'

'Good. I'm just waiting for two more staff members then we'll start the brief.'

'Harrison said there's been an emergency?' Amelia looked down at the hastily scribbled notes sitting beside the phone, trying to decipher them, but her mind was too full of what was happening around her. Everyone was grinning and smiling at them and Harrison was still holding her hand.

'Oh,' Rosie sighed dreamily as she entered the nurses' station. 'It's so nice to see you looking so happy, Harrison. You, too, Amelia.'

Tina edged closer and said softly, 'So I take it you're the boss's girlfriend.'

Amelia found it impossible to look at any of her colleagues, knowing that her cheeks were flaming red. She wasn't an openly demonstrative person and if she'd known holding hands with Harrison would have caused this much of a stir, she probably wouldn't have done it…probably.

'Oh, here they come,' Tina said, and the moment was broken, everyone returning to their professional personas. 'OK.' She held everyone's attention as she briefed them on the situation. 'Apparently, the rock concert being held on the foreshore got out of hand, the crowd going a little crazy with quite a few fights breaking out. At last count eight ambulances have been sent to the scene. We're going to have walk-ins, fractures, abrasions, lacerations, possible burns, not to mention people pumped up on alcohol and goodness knows what else.'

'I guess Saturday night *is* all right for fighting,' one nurse said to her friend, and they both laughed.

'Focus on your jobs, please.' Harrison's voice was quiet but firm. 'According to Tina, we're going to be inundated.' He spoke to everyone gathered. 'Work through each problem as it comes. If the patient isn't critical, patch them up and ship them off. They can come back tomorrow or see their GP on Monday. AJ, you and I'll be in treatment room one. Tina, put a team together and take treatment room two.' The wail of the ambulance siren broke the air and for a second everyone was still, as though waiting for a director to call, 'Action.' The next moment everyone was moving.

Amelia didn't have time to think about Harrison or anything else for the next three hours as they worked through one injury after another. She liked working side by side with Harrison and tonight they were definitely in tune with one another, pre-empting and assisting with little spoken communication.

Just after midnight, the patients were still coming, although a number of cases had been diverted to other hospitals. The police had also been called to the hospital to break up a fight that had started in the waiting room because there were so many people. The staff had tried to explain that it didn't matter in what order you arrived, patients were seen in priority order of their injuries.

Gina arrived, wheeling in a new patient. 'Who wants this young man?' she said.

'We're free,' Harrison called. Amelia came around him to the other side.

'Lift on three,' Harrison said. 'One, two, three.' They shifted the patient across as Gina gave a quick report.

'Nineteen-year-old male. Kevin Western. Half a pack a day smoker. Has had beer tonight, blood-alcohol reading is below point-oh-five. Sustained blunt force trauma to the right chest, with bruising and fractured T3 and T4. Patient is finding it difficult to breathe. Oxygen given. Possible pneumothorax.'

'Thanks, Gina.' Amelia pulled on a pair of gloves. 'Hi, Kevin. I'm Amelia. Can you talk?' She pressed her fingers to his wrist and found the pulse quite weak. Harrison was checking his pupils.

'No drugs tonight?' he asked, hooking his stethoscope into his ears and listened to Kevin's breathing.

'No,' Kevin said, his breathing laboured as his clothes were cut off and a blanket placed over him.

'There are no breath sounds on the right side and there's increased hyper-resonance,' Harrison stated for Amelia's sake before he had a closer look at the chest wound, touching it carefully.

'No time for X-ray?' Amelia asked.

'Exactly. Most likely scenario is that the fracture has punctured the lung, causing it to collapse.' Harrison looked at their patient while the nurses continued with the observations. 'Get it set up.'

Amelia nodded and went to the cupboard, pulling out a needle and valve tube as Harrison explained.

'When you were hit, your ribs broke and have poked a hole in your lung. That's why you're having trouble breathing. Your lung has collapsed due to a collection of air between the chest wall and the lung or the pleural cavity, as we like to call it. When you breathe out, some of that air is going into the pleural cavity. We need to insert a tube into your chest and then we can suck the air out.'

Kevin's eyes were wide with this news but Amelia wheeled a trolley over, smiled at him and administered a local anaesthetic.

'You'll be fine,' she reassured him. 'Once we've re-established the negative pressure within the cavity, the lung will expand again and you'll be able to breathe again. First, though, we need to elevate you a bit so just lie still. You're on the super-dooper bed, as we like to call it.' Amelia pressed a button and the bed started to rise, lifting Kevin up into more of a sitting position.

'Super-dooper?' Harrison asked as he ripped open the package which contained the needle. 'Is that the technical term back in England?'

Amelia's eyes twinkled with humour. 'Actually, it is.'

They were all starting to get a little light-hearted. It happened when they'd been going at it non-stop for a few hours but although they were all joking and happy, it didn't stop them from being serious about their work.

'Ready?' Harrison asked Kevin, and made a small incision into the pleural space. Amelia inserted the catheter through the second intercostal space, which would remove the air. The tube went down into an underwater-seal drainage bottle.

Harrison sutured the tube to the chest wall, then

stepped back so the nurse could cover it with an airtight dressing. The tubes were kept clamped while they performed the procedure and once it was done, they activated the drainage system.

Kevin was able to breathe a lot easier. 'There you go,' Amelia said to her patient, before turning to the nurse. 'See if there's any room in the men's ward. Kevin will need these drains in for at least the next twenty-four hours.' Amelia ripped off her gloves and looked across at Harrison. 'How much longer do you think this is going to go on?'

'I'm not sure but at least the patients aren't coming in as fast as they were a few hours ago.'

'Good point. Right. If we have no more ambulances coming in, I'll go grab a chart and see another patient.' It was another hour and a half later before A and E looked almost bare compared to the wall-to-wall people who had been there earlier. 'I'm going to get my bag and go home,' she said, smothering a yawn.

'Why don't you sit down for a minute?' Tina suggested.

'I can't. If I sit down, I doubt I'll get up again.' Amelia looked around her, assuming Harrison was with a patient.

'I haven't seen him,' Tina said.

'Pardon?'

'Harrison. I haven't seen him but I think he's still here.'

'Good, because he said he was going to walk me home. Or maybe after all of this he'd prefer to take a taxi.'

'Nah.' Tina shook her head. 'Tired or not, if he walks you home, he gets to spend more time with you.' She chuckled. 'The boss has it bad.'

'Bad what?'

'Bad for you, honey.'

'Don't say that,' Amelia groaned.

'Don't say what?' Harrison asked as he walked towards them.

'Um…nothing.' Amelia sat up straighter in her chair, not wanting him to know they'd been talking about him.

'I've got another patient here,' Rosie said, waving a file. 'Who wants her?'

'I'll do it.' Amelia stood, needing to get herself under control, and accepted the file. 'The sooner I start, the sooner I finish.'

'Thanks, Amelia. This poor woman has been waiting for two hours to be seen.'

Amelia went into cubicle three. 'I'm sorry you've been waiting so long, Ms Franklin.'

'It's OK,' the woman said. 'You've been busy.'

'Thank you for being so understanding.'

'I've had X-rays.'

'Oh? Let me find the packet.' Amelia went out to the nurses' station and hunted around.

'What are you looking for?' Harrison asked.

'Ms Franklin's X-rays.' Amelia yawned, tiredness swamping her. Harrison shifted pieces of paper and finally found them.

'Here you go.'

'Ah, thanks.' She hugged them to her chest.

'When you're done, will you be ready to leave?'

She smothered another yawn. 'Definitely.'

'Still OK if I walk you home?'

'Sure. I think I need some fresh air.'

'Good, then go see your patient and I'll make Tina take all the other cases.'

Amelia couldn't help smiling at his words as she returned to her patient. 'Here they are.' She flicked them up onto the viewing box and studied them. 'Your arm is definitely broken. Two hairline fractures as well. It says in your notes that you were pushed and when you fell, someone stood on your arm.'

'That's right. What a fun concert!' Her words were dripping with sarcasm and Amelia smiled.

'You've spoken to the police?'

'Yes. It won't do any good but at least I've done the right thing.'

'Good. A cast will fix that arm. You'll need to have it on for six weeks then make an appointment with either one of the orthopaedic surgeons here at the hospital or in their private practice. I'll leave a referral with the sister.'

'Thank you, Doctor.'

Amelia returned the X-rays to the nurses' station where Harrison was waiting for her, chatting with Rosie and Tina. Amelia wrote up Ms Franklin's notes as well as contacting the plaster nurse and writing the referral for the specialist.

'Ready?' Harrison asked.

'Just need to get my bag out of my locker.' Amelia hurried towards the change rooms and was back within a minute.

'Wow. That was quick. Eager to get out of here?' Tina asked.

'Most definitely.'

'All right. You two crazy kids go have a good time,' she joked, and Amelia simply rolled her eyes at her friend, ignoring the 'call-me' gesture Tina was making with her little finger and thumb.

'Goodnight, all,' Harrison said as they walked out of A and E. Once outside, he slipped his arm around her and she went willingly. Even though the early morning air was quite pleasant, it was a little cool. They'd made it out of the hospital gate and down to the street corner before he spoke. 'Aren't you going to say something?'

'Um.' Amelia cleared her throat. 'I'm not sure what to say.'

'I'm sorry if you feel uncomfortable under everyone's scrutiny.'

'They all seem very happy for you.'

Harrison shrugged. 'We've all known each other for a long time. Some of the staff I've worked with since I was a medical student, which was long before I met Inga or became a father. But let's forget the hospital. Now it's just you and me, out here, beneath the starry sky.'

Amelia was surprised at how right everything felt, although she did have a few questions. 'Well, let's just wait a minute on that.'

'On what?'

'On forgetting the hospital.'

'OK,' he drawled. 'What do you want to discuss?'

'How about the fact that everyone thinks I'm your girlfriend?'

Harrison looked down at her, a slow smile tugging at the corners of his lips. He glanced up and down the street, checking for traffic. They waited for a car to go before crossing over, the streetlights bright and illuminating the way for them.

'Aren't you?'

'Well, I don't know. I've been helping you out with Yolanda, you kissed me for the first time today—'

'Yesterday,' he corrected her, and she nodded, acquiescing.

'You kissed me yesterday and now you've held my

hand in public and the hospital thinks I'm your latest girlfriend.'

'Latest?' He seemed hurt by that. 'The last girlfriend I had ended up being my wife.'

'My point exactly.'

'It is?'

'Harrison, we can't get heavily involved. I don't mean to sound like a stuck record but I have a life back in England.'

He frowned and tightened his arm about her shoulders, not liking her words. 'I know that.'

'Then you must also realised this…thing…between us.' She shrugged. 'It can't go anywhere.'

'Why not?'

'Why not?' she asked with incredulity.

'Yes. Why not, AJ?'

'Because we live in different countries. Different continents!'

'Oh.' Was that the only reason she seemed so reticent? Was there more to it than that? She'd opened up to him, told him about her endometriosis, but was there more? His gut feeling said there was.

'Adding Yolanda to that equation provides an even stronger reason why we shouldn't.'

'Yet here you are, with your arm around me, walking down the street at two o'clock in the morning.'

'I'm not saying I don't like you—I do. Perhaps too much.'

'Well, why don't we start there and move forward?' Harrison suggested, now quite intrigued as to why she was fighting this so much.

'Because I have to finish this rotation, return to the other side of the world, study for my final exams and then, once I'm qualified, decide whether or not I'm going to take the job I've already been offered.'

'You've been offered a job?' He was stunned at this. 'In England?'

'Don't sound so surprised.'

'I didn't mean it that way. Of course you've been head-hunted. Why wouldn't you be? You're a fantastic doctor. I was just surprised because I hadn't realised that was the case.'

'There's so much we don't know about each other, Harrison.'

'Then we should at least be given the opportunity to find out.' They were walking past his darkened house but they continued on to her apartment. 'AJ, we have something very special between us and I can't seem to get you out of my mind. You've become important to me in a short space of time and when I'm with you I can't help but want to touch you, and when we're apart I wish I was with you, holding your hand, holding you in my arms, pressing my lips to yours.

'It's powerful. It's frightening and thrilling and it's growing so rapidly I think we'd be unable to stop it…if we wanted to, which I don't. I *want* to be with you, AJ. I don't know where it's going to lead or what might happen. All I know is I've never felt this way about anyone before.'

'Not even your wife?'

'No.' His answer was said without hesitation. 'She never made me feel as though I could fly, as though I could take on the world. You do. You bring out the best in me. I'd never intentionally hurt you, AJ. You're far too special.'

'I am?'

'You are.' They paused at her door and she withdrew her keys. Harrison realised he'd pushed enough for one night but that didn't mean he was going to stop seeing her. 'So, will I see you later today?'

'I want to sleep, then work. Perhaps tomorrow?'

'Meaning Monday?'

'Yes. I'm on day shift for the next two days, then off Wednesday and Thursday.'

'Right. Dinner? Tomorrow night?'

'Harrison…'

'Come on, AJ. It's just dinner. Mrs D. and Yolanda will be there. You know you want to see them.'

'OK,' she agreed reluctantly even though she knew she shouldn't. 'You'd better go.'

Harrison nodded and brushed his lips across hers. 'Sleep well.'

'Happy Easter.'

He jerked back and stared at her. 'It's Easter Sunday?'

'I know, hence the happy Easter comment.'

'I forgot to hide the eggs!'

'Have you bought them?'

'Mrs D. has.'

'Thank goodness those arrangements were left to her.'

Harrison shook his head, unable to believe he'd forgotten. 'I'd better go do that now before I try and move Yolanda out of my bed.'

'She sleeps in your bed?'

'I wasn't sure how late I'd be so I told Mrs D. to just let her sleep in there.' He shrugged. 'It relaxes her, helps her.'

'So you get to sleep in the pretty pink and white bed?' A smile touched her lips.

'Yes. Whoever said to buy your children good beds

with good mattresses because at some point you'll end up sleeping in them knew what they were talking about. I just hope she hasn't woken up.'

'Would Mrs D. have called you?'

'Yes, so as I haven't received a call, I'm presuming everything's all right.' He shook his head. 'Typical. The night I'm wide awake, she doesn't wake up.'

Amelia smiled. 'That's children for you. Go hide those eggs.'

'I will. I'll call you later,' he said and blew her a kiss. Amelia shut the door and leant against it, smiling, her heart filled with love for him.

Love!

Where had that thought come from? She stayed where she was, searching her thoughts and her heart for confirmation. Yes. It was true! She'd fallen in love with him. What was she to do?

CHAPTER NINE

WHEN she finally got to sleep that Easter Sunday morning, she had very sweet dreams, dreams of herself, Harrison and Yolanda playing happy families, although this time it was real. She was married to Harrison, Yolanda called her 'Mum' instead of 'Meel-ya' and her world was everything she'd ever dreamed of.

By the time she woke up, it was after lunch and she was glad she didn't have to go to work...or see Harrison. The realisation she was in love with him was too much for her to cope with at the moment as she hadn't expected it. To see him, to come face to face with him when her feelings felt as though they were going to overpower her... She started shaking at the thought.

She simply hadn't expected...hadn't *planned* to fall in love with him. Yolanda? Yes. She had no problem loving the child, it was impossible not to. She even had a fondness and respect for Mrs Deveraux, but falling in love with her boss? What had she been thinking?

'You weren't thinking,' Amelia whispered. Somehow Harrison had managed to break through her barriers, the ones she'd so carefully erected over the years. He'd broken through and managed to unlock her heart, the result being that she was now head over heels in love with him. She shook her head as the words repeated over and over. She loved him!

'I love Harrison,' she said out loud, looking at her reflection and knowing it was true. The emotion excited and overwhelmed her at the same time, but it also gave her clarity of mind. She knew what she had to do.

She had to make a break from the Stapleton family and the sooner she did it, the better it would be for all concerned. After she'd showered and had had something to eat, she decided to go for a walk along the beach. She needed to get out, to get some air, to find some control over her thoughts.

In an effort to avoid bumping into Harrison and his daughter, who might well be out playing on the beach, enjoying their chocolate Easter eggs, Amelia decided to walk south towards Brighton beach, away from Glenelg. Harrison had said Brighton was a nice beach so she should at least see it while she was there.

Harrison. Everything seemed to come back to Harrison.

When she opened her door to leave, she was flabbergasted to find a present propped up on the wall by her door. An envelope was attached with her name written on it—it was definitely for her. She glanced around, expecting to see someone standing there, delivering it, but there was no one about. How long had it been there?

Hesitantly, she took it inside and withdrew the card. It simply said, 'Happy Easter and a very big thank you for all your help.' It was signed by Yolanda, Mrs Deveraux and Harrison, the child having done a very good job at writing her own name but she'd obviously had some help. She'd also put three very big 'kisses' at the bottom of the card and Amelia couldn't help but smile.

How on earth was she going to extract herself from such a darling? It would be painful, more so for her than for Yolanda, because Amelia knew she didn't want to do it. She wanted to be a part of Yolanda's life, to watch her grow and change and to be there to experience those changes. She yearned for it…and that was the reason she had to stop it. It couldn't happen.

Amelia put the card down and turned her attention to the present. With trembling fingers she carefully removed the wrapping paper, folding it neatly, her heart filling with new love at the framed photograph of the pretty princess palace they'd sculpted on the beach. It was the most perfect present and she hung the picture in her room so it was the last thing she could look at before she went to sleep.

Harrison had done it again and she hated him for his thoughtfulness. It only made what she had to do even harder. She knew she'd take that picture back to England with her and it would always remind her of the flawless morning they'd had breakfast on the beach…the morning Harrison had kissed her for the first time.

Amelia closed her eyes, pain searing her heart. Why was this so difficult?

'Because you're in love with the man, you idiot,' she said out loud, and stormed to the door, deciding a run along the beach was going to be more beneficial than a walk. She needed to get these emotions under control, and fast.

She tossed and turned that night and the next morning went to work, glad it was a public holiday and Harrison had decided to stay home with his family. Still, as she went about treating patients and talking to staff, she was starting to dread seeing him for dinner that evening.

Oh, she wanted to see him. She wanted to see him

more than anything; she wanted him to hold her again, to kiss her again, to hear him call her beautiful... But it was wrong. It was a lie to let him think they could continue to spend time together because they simply couldn't. Perhaps if she hadn't fallen in love with him she could have continued to enjoy his company, as well as Yolanda's, but that wasn't the way things had worked out.

Three times she picked up a house phone and dialled his number...well, all but the last digit...before she replaced it. The least Harrison deserved was for her to tell him face to face that she couldn't continue to be involved with him. The problem was, every time she looked into his eyes she melted and her mind went blank.

On the way home from work, she picked up a bottle of wine for dinner and a drawing set for Yolanda. It contained pink and white paper and coloured pencils, all wrapped up in a box with a pink bow. It was perfect for her. She also bought a new book by one of Mrs D.'s favourite authors and then realised she didn't have anything for Harrison.

She hadn't intentionally been buying presents but now it would look strange if she gave something to Yolanda and Mrs D. and had nothing for Harrison. Well, it probably wasn't a good idea to give him a present when she was going to break up with him...even though they'd hardly begun.

Amelia dressed with care, wearing a blue knit top with matching jacket and a pair of casual black trousers. Gathering up her parcels, she took her camera with her, determined to punish herself further by taking photographs of this, their last evening together. She was trembling as she rang his doorbell and when she heard his footsteps heading in her direction, she took a few deep breaths, trying to calm her nerves.

'AJ,' he said, and ushered her inside. He closed the door then stopped to look at her. 'You look beautiful.'

'Thanks,' she muttered, trying to stay detached. Unsure what to do next, she held out the bottle of wine.

'Thank you.' Harrison accepted it, wanting to kiss her, even if it was just for a moment, but there was something about the way she stood, clutching parcels to her chest, that told him she wasn't comfortable with that idea. 'Come on through. Yolanda's very excited you're—'

He broke off as little footsteps came running in her direction and a second later Yolanda had her arms wrapped around her Meel-ya's legs. 'I done lots and lots wif Daddy today. We did da drwawing, da dancing, da *dollies.*'

'Sounds as though you've had a very busy day,' Amelia replied, as she shuffled through to the kitchen.

'Is dat mine?' Yolanda's eyes caught on the pink present in Amelia's hands.

'How did you guess?'

'Is pi-i-in-n-nk.' The little eyes grew round with delight.

'Why don't you sit up at the bench and you can open it?' Yolanda scrambled up onto the chair and then held her arms out. Amelia handed the present over. The paper was ripped and discarded and then oohs and ahhs came from Yolanda as she touched the pink and white paper.

Amelia glanced at Harrison to find him smiling at her. 'What do you say?' he prompted his daughter.

'Tank-oo, Meel-ya,' Yolanda immediately replied.

'Why don't you take that into your bedroom and you can do some drawing while Daddy finishes getting dinner ready?'

'O-tay.' Yolanda scrambled down again, collected her prize and ran to her room. Now that they were alone,

Amelia felt the atmosphere around them change. Harrison touched her arm and she turned to look at him, sucking in a breath at his caress.

He saw the same hesitation in her eyes, felt it in the way she tensed and realised something had changed since he'd kissed her goodbye early the previous morning.

'Everything all right?' He dropped his hand and went around the bench into the kitchen, lifting the lid on a saucepan and stirring its contents.

'Uh…yes.'

'Busy day?'

'It wasn't too bad.' Work. She all but sighed with relief at the topic. It was neutral. 'We had a steady stream of patients, a few stomachaches due to too much food or too much bad food. We had a child who was dressed in a superhero costume who'd cracked his head on a slide and sustained a mild concussion.'

'Did it need suturing?'

'No. I was able to just seal it with superglue.'

'Appropriate for a superhero.'

'I thought so.' Amelia sat down on a stool and watched him move around the kitchen. He was more than competent and she allowed herself a moment of pleasure at falling in love with a man who seemed good at everything. 'Smells delicious,' she said.

'Hungarian goulash, mashed potatoes, corn on the cob and green beans.'

'Mmm, sounds delicious, and here I was expecting chocolate bread, chocolate soup and chocolate cake for dessert.'

'Ugh. I think we've all definitely had enough chocolate after yesterday.'

'How did Yolanda cope?'

'We managed to restrict her to one small Easter egg per hour and she broke her big one up for dessert.'

'Sugar high?'

'Yes, although she wasn't too bad.' Harrison paused then looked at Amelia. 'We, uh…went around to your place yesterday afternoon but you weren't there.'

'No.'

She didn't provide any more details and again Harrison was left feeling there was something important she wasn't telling him. 'Yolanda wanted to show you her Easter eggs.'

'I'm sorry I missed them.'

'You…uh…weren't called in, were you?'

'No.' She could sense he was about to ask her where she'd been and so decided to quickly change the subject. 'I take it Mrs D.'s resting?'

'Yes. She'll be out soon.'

'She's doing well?'

'Better than well. The woman heals quite quickly for someone her age.'

'I heard that,' Mrs Deveraux said as she walked into the room, leaning on her cane for support. 'You rotten child,' she joked.

Harrison smiled and Amelia took a mental picture of it. He was so handsome. 'Child? I'm hardly that.'

'Harrison Stapleton, I've known you since you were younger than Yolanda and that makes you a child in my book.'

'Speaking of books,' Amelia said as Mrs D. perched herself on a stool beside her. 'This is for you.' She handed over the present. 'I thought it would give you a good excuse to sit down and put your feet up.'

'Thank you, dear. That's very thoughtful of you.' The woman carefully took the paper off.

'Just rip it,' Harrison said.

'No,' Amelia and Mrs D. said in unison, and he laughed, rolling his eyes.

'The paper's too pretty to rip,' Mrs D. said, and then gasped with delight at seeing the title of the book. 'Oh, Amelia. I doubt I'm going to get through dinner. I want to go lock myself away right now and read it.'

'Eat first,' Harrison said, hoping Mrs D. would do just as she'd suggested. He could get Yolanda into bed and then he and Amelia could have some quiet time, just talking and being with each other. 'I'm ready to dish up.'

'I'll set the table,' Mrs D. said, but Amelia made her sit down.

'No. You rest. I can do it.' Amelia went into the kitchen, mindful of keeping her distance from Harrison as she collected the cutlery. He called Yolanda and soon they were all sitting, Harrison at one end of the table and Amelia at the other. Mrs Deveraux had insisted she sit there and once more it made Amelia feel as though she was back in happy family land. The food was delicious, the atmosphere was relaxed and she couldn't help pulling out her camera to capture it all. She would need more than just her memory to get her through and even if it hurt to look at the photographs, hopefully one day, in years to come, she would be able to remember this most precious time spent with the man she loved.

Yolanda, naturally, posed for her pictures, grinning with delight, and as Amelia took a snap of the child sitting on her father's knee, a lump formed in her throat which was difficult to swallow. Breaking away from them was going to be far harder than she'd realised.

After dinner, she took the opportunity to get some

space from Harrison and volunteered to supervise Yolanda's bathtime.

She'd knelt beside the bathtub and watched with delight the way Yolanda made her bath toys talk to each other, exactly the same way she did with the dolls. 'You tate turtle,' Yolanda said, handing over an orange turtle.

'What's the turtle's name?'

'Mr Turtle,' Yolanda said, rolling her eyes as though 'Meel-ya' was silly not to know that. They continued to play in the water and once she was done, Amelia towelled her dry and then to her surprise the little girl ran, squealing, in all her nakedness through the house to her bedroom.

'She loves doing that,' Mrs D. said with a laugh as she headed towards her own bedroom. 'Goodnight, dear.' She patted the book under her arm. 'I doubt I'll be seeing you again this evening.'

Amelia smiled. 'Enjoy it.' She followed Yolanda and managed to get her dressed in her pretty pink nightie and then sat at the top of the bed, while Yolanda snuggled beneath the pink and white covers, to read her a story.

Three stories later, Amelia wondered if the child was ever going to show signs of tiredness. Then, to her surprise, Yolanda turned and put her arm over Amelia's waist, yawning as she did so.

'I wuv you, Meel-ya,' she said, and closed her eyes.

Amelia's heart constricted with pain and love as she gazed down at the child. 'I love you, too,' she whispered, and knew it was impossible to blink back the tears. Her heart swelled with such love, such protectiveness and such devotion as she stroked the little blonde curls. This child meant the world to her and Amelia knew with certainty that she never wanted to be parted from her…but she *had* to.

'Why is this so hard?' She brushed away the tears that had rolled down her cheeks.

'Why is what so hard?' Harrison asked softly from the doorway, and Amelia looked up. He stayed where he was for a moment before crossing quietly to kiss his daughter's cheek. 'She's such an angel when she sleeps,' he murmured.

'She's an angel all the time,' Amelia added.

'Then why are you crying?' He held out his hand to help her up and she hesitated for a second before accepting it. It would be the last time, she told herself. The last time she would allow herself to touch him, yet when she tried to remove her hand he held on, leading her from the room. Neither of them spoke a word until they were settled in the lounge, the table lamps on and soothing music coming through the stereo.

The whole atmosphere screamed romance and Amelia resisted sitting down until Harrison tugged her down beside him, still holding her hand. He turned it over in his, smoothing his fingers over her palm, his touch slow and intimate. Why? Oh, why was he doing this to her?

She found it difficult to look at him and remained perched on the edge of the seat, unable to relax. She knew what she needed to do, knew it was the right thing, but being with him like this, the love in her heart powering through her like a drug, it was almost impossible to resist… But resist she must.

'AJ?' She was having trouble looking at him and he sensed something was wrong. He only wished she'd open up and tell him. 'What's wrong?'

'Oh, Harrison.' Her breathing wild with panic, she wrenched her hand free of his and rose to her feet. He followed her, thinking she was about to bolt, but instead she wrung her hands together and looked about the room. 'I can't do this.'

He put his hands on her shoulders and turned her to face him. 'Can't do what? What do you mean?'

'This! You and I. I can't be your…girlfriend.'

'Why not? It's all right, Amelia-Jane.' He tried to gather her close but she resisted and he dropped his hands. 'I thought we agreed? We agreed to see where this attraction we feel for each other leads.'

'No. *You* agreed, Harrison. I put up a protest.'

'You said you were leaving at the end of June. I know that. You know that.'

'Then why are you continuing to pursue me? This has catastrophe written all over it and I can't do this to her.'

'To who? Yolanda?'

'Yes. I need to start withdrawing. It's only fair. Mrs D. is fine. You yourself said she was progressing better than you'd anticipated and although you may need a bit of help, it's not that much. I can come over and spend a few hours with Yolanda, gradually weaning that time down over the next few weeks.'

'So that's it? Just like that?'

'It's the right thing to do.'

'For who? For Yolanda? Or for yourself? Because it's certainly not the right thing to do as far as I'm concerned, but we seem to be leaving my feelings on this matter out of the equation.' He stepped closer and she breathed in his warm scent and almost sighed with longing. 'When do we discuss what's between us, Amelia? I don't care if you live here or in England or in Timbuktu, these feelings I have for you are real and honest and I won't let you just run roughshod over them, giving me some trumped-up reason why you have to end it.'

'It's not trumped up,' she said, trying to keep control over her senses, but it was proving difficult when he was so close.

'Then why can't you let go? Why can't you admit what's between us? Why can't you trust me enough to tell me what's really wrong?'

'Because I'll get hurt.' The words were wrenched from her and Harrison heard her pain. He'd realised there was more to her wanting to withdraw and he'd been trying to figure out what it was. Now, at least, she'd confirmed there was something, but what? He was positive that once he knew what he was dealing with, he'd be able to fix it.

'How will you get hurt, AJ? Certainly not by me.'

There was no way she could explain. To tell him she might not be able to have children… She couldn't even form the words, let alone get them past her lips. 'Please, Harrison. Let me go.'

'I can't.' To prove his point, he lowered his mouth to hers, capturing her in an electrifying kiss. The more he touched her, the more he craved her, and the more he craved her, the more he realised his life would never be the same again.

She clung to him and he felt her need, felt her response, and instantly knew this wasn't the reason she wanted to make a clean break from him. The power and the passion between them was incredible and right. Surely she could feel that. Surely she realised this sort of thing didn't happen every day. So why was she saying she couldn't be with him? They broke apart, both panting, Amelia limp and luscious in his arms.

'You've changed my life, Amelia-Jane. You've changed Yolanda's. I don't find it easy to trust anyone, especially not with Yolanda, but I trust you and that is so rare. Yolanda adores you, she loves you.'

'I know and I love her.'

'Then why? Why pull back? You're so natural with her. The love you have for her is everything her mother should have given but didn't. My daughter needs you, AJ, and so do I.'

With a sob Amelia shifted out of his arms and took three steps away. 'Don't make this more difficult than it already is.'

'I will. I'll fight for you. I'll show you that what we have is worth the fight. First, though, you need to tell me what's really wrong. You need to trust me.'

Amelia bit her lip, her breathing was so fast she felt as though her lungs were about to pop or that she'd pass out from lack of oxygen. She knew he was right. She at least owed him the truth and she knew once he found out, he wouldn't want her any more. And it was that pain, that searing pain, that would tear her heart apart and which she was trying to avoid.

'Is this because of your endometriosis?' he asked suddenly, and she gasped. It was what he needed. It gave him the clue that he was on the right path and his brain started working overtime, piecing everything together, everything he knew about her. 'You feel that you being sick every now and then might put a strain on our relationship?'

He watched her face closely, trying to read her expression. He'd definitely hit on the right topic. 'You've had an ovary and a Fallopian tube removed. Does that mean…?' He stopped, the light going on in his head, and he saw the fear in her eyes, the fear that he had indeed discovered the truth. 'You might not be able to have children,' he stated softly, and his heart turned over with compassion at the pain she must be feeling. He saw the truth of his statement reflected within her and couldn't believe how deeply he felt for her. 'You're so wonderful with Yolanda and yet you might be denied the opportunity to have any of your own.'

Tears started running down her cheeks at his words and Harrison moved towards her, only to have her back away instantly.

'AJ, stop. Don't run from me. Let's talk about this.' Harrison held out his hand, waiting for her to take it, to accept the help he was offering. She'd accepted it earlier when he'd helped her up from Yolanda's bed but he doubted she'd accept it this time, despite how much he was willing her to do exactly that.

She sidestepped over to the doorway. 'I can't.' She shook her head, adding emphasis to her words. 'I can't, Harrison. I won't do that to you, to Yolanda. I can't.'

With that, she turned and headed towards the front door. Harrison followed her, not willing to let her walk out of his life.

'Amelia-Jane,' he called, his voice louder than he'd anticipated, and in the next instant he heard Yolanda start to cry. He gritted his teeth, ignoring his daughter for a moment as he chased after Amelia. 'Please. Let's talk about this.'

She opened the front door and stepped through before turning to face him. 'There's nothing to talk about, Harrison.' She shook her head sadly. 'It's over.'

CHAPTER TEN

THERE was a knock at Harrison's office door and he put his pen down, glad his registrar had finally answered her pager. 'Come in,' he called, and a moment later Tina came through the door.

'You wanted to see me, boss?'

'I did. Sit down, Tina.'

Tina settled herself in the chair opposite him. 'So? What's up?'

'Amelia.'

'Oh.' Tina went to stand again but he stopped her.

'Wait. Please.' His tone was imploring with a hint of desperation. 'Come on, Tina. Talk to me. Tell me what's going on.'

'You need to ask Amelia that. I'm Switzerland.'

'Then why have you been swapping shifts with her?'

'Switzerland can help people in need and still remain neutral, you know. Remember those Von Trapp children, hiking over the mountains at the end of the movie?'

'What are you talking about?'

'Switzerland is just there, doing what it needs to do, and if people come hiking over their mountains, well…then that's OK.'

'Which means you should be able to help me as well. Can't show favouritism to one and not the other.'

Tina frowned. 'Good point.' She smiled at him. 'OK, boss, what do you need?'

'I need information. I need you to tell me why Amelia isn't returning my calls, why she never seems to be in her apartment, why she keeps switching her shifts. Every time I try to contact her, I'm thwarted.'

'You saw her yesterday. I distinctly remember the two of you working with a patient who was looking a horrible shade of green.'

Harrison couldn't believe the way he'd felt at seeing Amelia. It had been like the sun had started shining through the dark, stormy clouds that had been dogging him for the past few weeks. She'd looked fresh and gorgeous and her scent had overpowered him, but he'd had no time to talk, to do anything other than focus on the patient. He frowned as he recalled what had happened next.

'Yes, and then the patient turned a more normal-looking colour after he'd emptied the contents of his stomach all over my trousers,' he growled. 'By the time I'd changed and returned to A and E, AJ had gone.' Harrison stood and raked a hand through his hair.

Tina shrugged. 'It was the end of her shift.'

'Come on. Take pity on me, Tina. Why won't she talk to me?'

'What do you think is the reason?'

'I think it's because I've discovered her secret. I think it's because I got too close and now she's running. If she could finish her rotation tomorrow, she'd be on the next plane back to Heathrow. Too bad, Harrison. Too bad, Yolanda.'

'Yolanda? I thought she'd been spending time with Yolanda.'

'She has and she's been weaning herself slowly out of my life in the process. It isn't working. Yolanda is still asking where Amelia is, wanting to spend more and more time with her. I gave Amelia space because I thought she needed it. I thought once she'd had a chance to think things through that she'd at least *talk* to me, be polite, friendly, but she's avoiding me like the plague and it's just going too far. I don't even know what shift she's on and I'm the one who does the rosters!'

'You know I'm not the one you're supposed to be talking to.'

'I know that but she's become as slippery as an eel.'

Tina watched him for a moment and he knew he was under close scrutiny. What did she see? Did she see a man about to tip over the edge because he couldn't get two seconds alone with the woman he loved? That was certainly how he felt. Finally, Tina nodded. 'You're serious about her?'

He met her gaze, hope bubbling up through his despair. 'Dead serious.'

'What time do you finish tonight?'

'Five o'clock, or probably more around four-thirty. Yolanda has a therapy appointment.'

'Amelia's doing a late afternoon.'

He checked the roster. 'But that's what she's down to do.'

'I know. She figures you'll be gone, taking care of Yolanda. She knows your routine, Harrison, which makes it easy for her to dodge you.'

'So she'll be here just after five.'

'Can you hang around?'

'I'll make sure of it.' He nodded to Tina. 'Thanks, Switz, ol' pal.'

Tina grinned. 'Don't mention it, boss…and I *mean* don't mention it. I think the two of you are perfect for each other, which, by the way, is what I've been telling her.'

'Good. Nice to know I have an ally.'

'Just keep my name out of any reunion speeches.'

'You've got it.' He laughed as Tina left, beginning to feel as though an enormous weight had been lifted from his shoulders. So…Amelia would be in the hospital after five. He picked up the phone and rang Yolanda's therapist to see if he could delay her appointment an hour. That way, Yolanda wouldn't need to hang around as long and she'd be able to see her 'Meel-ya' when she had finished her session. Once that was organised, he called Mrs D. to let her know about the change.

Sitting back in his chair, he dragged in a deep, cleansing breath. He would convince Amelia. Before the day was done, he would convince Amelia-Jane Watson that he was the man for her. He loved her so completely that he was willing to fight every objection she threw at him in order to prove to her they were meant to be together— for ever. He would tell her everything in his heart.

He wasn't quite sure exactly when he'd fallen for his English registrar. All he knew was that it had been hard and irrefutable. She was the perfect woman for him. Yolanda loved her, Mrs D. thought the world of her, and together they would make one perfectly happy family.

Amelia walked to the change rooms and wearily opened her locker. She was exhausted and she knew it was due to her lack of sleep during the past fortnight, but work was what she was living for at the moment. She came, she worked until she was ready to drop and then could finally manage to sleep for a few hours, before waking up in a cold sweat, shaking with fear and loneliness, and sometimes calling Harrison's name.

She closed her eyes for a moment, unable to believe just how much she missed him. Her heart was breaking, she knew that, but she also knew it was better to break it now than let things get more out of control. Whoever had said that absence made the heart grow fonder hadn't been wrong. Her self-imposed exile from Harrison was only making her love him all the more.

She knew he'd tried to contact her and she'd gone to great lengths to avoid him, but deep down inside it was the last thing she wanted to do. Spending time with Yolanda had been the only bright spot in her days and now she'd cut it back to every second day and only when Harrison wasn't around.

Mrs Deveraux had tried to talk to her, tried to get her to open up, but Amelia had refused to be swayed from her purpose. She'd come to Australia to do her job, not to fall in love. So many years of hard work would be flushed down the drain if she couldn't get through these next few weeks.

'Hey, there,' Tina said, and Amelia jumped, spinning around to look at her friend. 'Whoa. You look horrible.' She placed her hand on Amelia's forehead. 'No. You're not hot. You're not coming down with this virus that's going around, are you?'

'I'm fine, Tina.'

'Yeah, right. Like I really believe you.'

Amelia closed her locker, hooked her stethoscope around her neck and pinned on her ID badge. 'Leave it, please.'

'Leave what? I'm not going to have a dig at you or lecture you. I am, however, becoming quite concerned. You look as though you're in pain.'

'I am—and I'm not talking about my heart,' she added quickly. 'I forgot to take my meds a few days ago and now I'm paying for it.'

'But it's under control, right? I don't need to get the chief gynae down here, do I?'

'No. I'm fine. I'm used to controlling it myself and I'm feeling better today than yesterday. I had horrible pains when I went home from work.'

'Hmm.' Tina nodded as though she didn't believe her.

Amelia frowned. 'What's that supposed to mean?'

'Nothing. I promised I wasn't going to start.'

'You already have.' Amelia crossed her arms. 'Go on, then. Continue.'

'Well, it's just that yesterday you saw Harrison. That's all I was going to say.'

'So you think that because I saw him I was in more pain yesterday when I left work.'

'Yes.'

'Stomach pain. Not heart pain.'

Tina shrugged. 'Whatever! Look, why can't you at least give him five minutes…or possibly ten, just so he can talk to you.'

Amelia shook her head and walked towards the door. 'This is you not starting?'

'He's in pain, too, Amelia, and he doesn't suffer from endometriosis…at least, I sincerely hope he doesn't.'

Amelia couldn't help the smile that sprang easily to her lips at her friend's words. She could never stay mad at Tina for long.

'He misses you, Amelia.' Tina was serious.

'I know.'

'Then why can't you do something about it? You're good together, you two. Don't go throwing away something that could fulfil all your dreams.'

Amelia nodded, deciding she didn't have the energy to get into a discussion with Tina about what her dreams really were. 'Noted. I need to get to work.' She headed out to the nurses' station and picked up a set of case notes, glad she had things to occupy her mind other than visions of Harrison and how incredible it felt when he held her close.

Ten minutes after she'd started, she put a blood sample she'd just taken into a packet and spoke to the triage sister on duty. 'I need a rush on this so I'm going to take it to Pathology myself. We're quiet enough here at the moment but page me if anything urgent comes in. I shouldn't be too long.'

'Righto, Amelia,' the sister replied.

Amelia was pleased to get out of the hustle and bustle of staff, walking down the long grey corridor that would eventually lead to the pathology labs. Staff were turning off lights, closing offices, eager to get home for the night. It was now the end of April and the weather had turned from warm and summery to cool and pre-wintry in a matter of weeks. She didn't mind in the slightest as the earlier sunset and colder nights fitted with her mood at the moment. Bleak and depressing.

She delivered the sample to Pathology and then headed back, amazed at how in a matter of minutes corridors that had been busy with staff were now vacant. As Sister hadn't paged her, she decided to take the long way back to A and E and had just entered the southern stairwell when a man came hurtling up the stairs.

Amelia flattened herself against the wall to let him pass, but balked when she saw who it was.

'Harrison!'

'Oh, AJ. There you are. Thank God you're still here.' He closed his eyes for a second and she saw the pain and agitation on his face.

'What's wrong?' A feeling of dread washed over her. 'Yolanda?'

He nodded and reached for her hand, tugging her up the stairs. 'She's missing.'

'Oh, no.' They came out into the corridor Amelia had just come down. 'She's not down there,' she told him quickly. 'I've just come along this way.'

'Right.' He spun her around, still holding her hand, and took her back down the stairs.

Amelia was too overcome with worry for Yolanda to even bother trying to keep her distance from him. He needed her now and, despite what was happening between them, she would support him in any way she could. Yolanda was missing! Her gorgeous little girl was missing!

When they came out of the stairwell, Amelia pulled him to a stop but he didn't let go of her hand. It was as though she were his lifeline, giving him strength, and that made her feel vitally important to him. It was a nice feeling. 'Wait. We should split up. Where was she last seen?'

'She was at her therapy appointment. That's on level three.'

'She was having therapy at this time of night?'

'I changed her appointment,' he said, guilt swamping him as he'd changed it so he could see Amelia, but now was not the time to go into that. 'I went to collect her and the therapist came out of the room as I walked up and she was looking for Yolanda then. She said she'd only turned her back for a minute.'

'That's all it would take. Yolanda's very quick.'

'And stubborn.'

'You've searched level three?'

'Yes. I thought she might have headed down to A and E but no one's seen her there.'

'What about the lifts? She might be in the lifts. You know how much she likes pressing the buttons.'

'Yes. I hadn't thought of that.'

'You check the lifts. I'll go between A and E and the third floor. Last time I found her, she was in a dark corner, crying, so we'll need to check everywhere.'

'The therapist is looking, too, so you might bump into her.'

'OK.' Amelia gave his hand a little reassuring squeeze before saying firmly, 'We'll find her.'

'We have to, AJ.'

'We will.'

They parted, going their separate ways, Amelia's heart pounding with fear in her chest as she prayed nothing would happen to the child. Yolanda was so strong-willed and stubborn that if she got it into her head to do something, she did it. The problem now was once she realised she was lost, she would then become afraid and start crying. Amelia thought back to the first time she'd seen her, crouched low with tears on her face, and her heart churned with worry.

She searched, almost willing Yolanda to jump out of a shadow as though they were playing a game…but she didn't. 'Yolanda?' she called, but her voice simply echoed down the corridor.

Amelia rounded the corner that led towards the wards

on the third floor, her gaze scanning everything. She checked every door. Most of them were locked so Yolanda couldn't have got inside.

'Yolanda?' she heard someone else call, and a moment later a small woman dressed in a suit came into view and Amelia guessed it was the therapist.

'Any sign?' Amelia asked.

'No. You looking for her, too?'

'Yes.'

'She's not around here.'

Amelia sighed heavily and shook her head. 'Can you tell me what happened just before she disappeared? Did she say anything? Do anything? Did she need to go to the toilet?'

'No, she'd just been and I'd taken her myself. I was sitting down, talking to her and playing games like we always do. The phone rang and I stood to answer it. I swear I had my back turned for all of a minute and when I turned back, she was gone. Just like that!' The woman snapped her fingers. 'At first I thought she was hiding so I checked the cupboards and under the chairs and tables but there was no sign of her.'

'That took how long?'

'What?'

'How long were you looking for her in the room?'

'About a minute.'

'A three-year-old can cover a lot of distance in a minute.'

'Who are you?' the therapist asked. 'We haven't been introduced.'

'Dr Watson. I work in A and E with Harrison. What game were you playing before she left?'

'Tea parties. Her favourite.'

Amelia nodded. She'd played tea parties with Yolanda just that morning when she'd visited. She thought hard. 'Did she say anything? Was she going to get a doll? Another toy to join in?'

'Wait a second. She mumbled something about… Meel-ya? I don't know what that means.'

At that, Amelia felt the colour drain out of her.

'Are you all right, Dr Watson? You look very pale.'

'She was looking for me.' The words were a shocked whisper. 'I'm Amelia.'

'Oh.'

'She would have headed towards A and E but I've looked everywhere between there and here.' Amelia looked behind her as though expecting to see the child but the corridor was empty. 'No. She's not here.' She sighed and thought, trying to get into the three-year-old's mindset. If she hadn't been able to find Amelia, where would she have gone?

'Has anyone checked the children's ward?'

'I think Harrison called the ward sister and asked her to call him if she saw Yolanda.'

'I'll go check,' Amelia said. 'You keep looking around here, head towards A and E.'

'OK.'

Amelia raced for the stairwell, taking the steps two at a time, her heart pounding wildly. Yolanda loved the 'zoo' and hopefully, as she hadn't been able to find Amelia, she'd simply gone there to play, to get another toy to join in her tea party.

Bursting from the stairwell, she turned right, her gaze fixed on the brightly painted children's ward. If the ward sister was on the lookout and hadn't contacted Harrison, there was no point talking to her. Amelia needed to see for herself, however, that Yolanda hadn't somehow managed to get into the 'zoo' without the 'zoo-keeper' knowing.

Amelia walked to the playroom area and stopped at the gate, which required an adult to open it. There were four children in there, a couple playing together, the others playing by themselves. Amelia scanned the area quickly, her heart plummeting when she didn't immediately see Yolanda.

Where was she? Worry gripped her so tightly she felt ill and thought she might pass out. Nothing could happen to that child. Nothing! She loved her so much, needed her as much as she needed Yolanda's father.

Now the thought of returning to England, of not being able to see Yolanda or Harrison, of constantly wondering if they were all right…the thought made her head ache and her heart break. What had she done? Had she made the biggest mistake of her life in trying to extract herself from their lives? She loved them, loved Harrison so very much.

Tears blurred her vision as she gripped the bars of the security gate. She had to find her girl… If she didn't…if something had happened to Yolanda… Amelia shook her head and sniffed, forcing her mind back from that dark place. She needed to keep her head, to help Harrison search. She hoped he'd contacted hospital security because they also needed someone to keep watch outside the hospital…just in case.

She went to go but as she moved, a little pink leg caught her eye and she looked more closely. Two little pink legs, a child lying on the floor, but there were too many things obscuring her vision for her to see clearly.

Amelia fumbled with the latch on the gate but finally had it undone and rushed over, almost tripping over another child in her haste.

'Yolanda?' She called, and the child sat up, turning a tear-stained face towards her.

'Meel-ya!' Yolanda was on her feet, rushing towards her, and in the next instant she was caught in Amelia's arms.

'Oh, baby, baby. We were so worried. We couldn't find you.' Tears of joy poured down Amelia's cheeks as Yolanda clung to her.

'I not pind you, Meel-ya. Where you go?' Fresh tears came from the child and Amelia's heart lurched with love and longing.

'I'm here, darling. I'm here and I'm never going to let you go.'

'What's all this noise?' the ward sister said, coming to the gate, but she stopped when she saw Amelia holding Yolanda. 'Oh, my goodness, you've found her. I'll call Harrison.'

'Thanks,' Amelia said as the sister rushed off. She sat down in one of the chairs, not sure her legs could hold her any longer. She gathered the child to her, settling her on her lap. 'Daddy and I were so worried. We couldn't find you, darling.'

'I no pind you, Meel-ya.' Now that the scare had passed, Yolanda was starting to return to her usual stubborn self. 'Where you go?' she demanded.

'I'm right here and you found me now.'

'And you pound me, too.'

'Yes, I did. We found each other.' Amelia kissed her cheek.

'You no go again,' she said crossly.

'No. I won't go away again.'

'Oh, my darling girl.' A deep voice came from behind them and Yolanda instantly shifted from Amelia to launch herself at her father. 'My baby. Daddy was so worried.'

'Meel-ya worwied, too.'

'Yes, I'm sure she was.' He shifted Yolanda on his hip as Amelia stood and he looked at her. 'I heard what you said, AJ. Is it true? I won't have you lie to me or my daughter. Did you mean it when you said you wouldn't go away again?'

Amelia looked at him and slowly nodded. 'I can't leave her.'

'So you're saying you'll stay? Be a part of her life?'

'I'll be a part of her life while I'm here.' She shrugged. 'We'll just have to figure out some way to explain to her that I need to return to England.'

'And after England? After you've sat your finals?'

Amelia shrugged again. 'I don't know, Harrison.'

'I play in da zoo,' Yolanda said, and squirmed out of Harrison's arms to go and finish lining up the soft toy animals she loved playing with.

'Uh…has everyone else been told to stop looking?' Amelia asked, feeling highly self-conscious under Harrison's stare.

'Yes. AJ…' He paused and opened his arms. 'I need to hold you.'

She sighed and went willingly into his arms. After the tension they'd been through it was what they both needed, to simply stop and be with each other. It was where she loved being the most, close to Harrison, listening to his heart beating firmly.

'I love you, Amelia-Jane,' he said, tightening his hold

on her. 'Yolanda ended up getting in there first, but I was the one who was supposed to ask you to stay, to be a part of my life as well as hers. I can't let you go.'

Amelia had stilled at his words, knowing without a doubt they were true. 'I need to return to England.' She forced herself to ease back but he refused to let her go, only loosening his arms a little. 'I have exams.'

'I know.' He looked deep into her eyes. 'Amelia-Jane, I want you to marry me. I wanted to tell you earlier, that's why Yolanda and I were here. It's not gone quite the way I planned it, but…'

'Oh!' She didn't know what to do, what to say, and she started to tremble. It was all too much. How could he want to marry her when she couldn't provide him with what he needed? 'But—'

'But you can't have children?' He shrugged. 'I accept that.'

'Harrison you don't und—'

'I do understand. I understand *completely*.' He paused for effect, hoping his words were sinking in. 'I. Love. You. *You*. The sooner you realise and accept that, the sooner we can get on with our lives. I understand that you've been frustrated and angry for many years about your endometriosis. You had no say in it, no control over it, and you have a right to your feelings, but it isn't the be all and end all of your existence.'

His words were heartfelt, imploring and totally sincere. 'I need to be with you, AJ. The past few weeks have shown me that to try and live without you…well, it's not living at all, it's merely existing. There was an emptiness, a loneliness in my life, one I didn't realise I had until I met you. You filled that gap, you made me whole. We have Yolanda and that's enough. We can adopt, if that's what you'd like. We can try IVF if that's your choice. Hear those words—*your* choice. You've looked at this with only one perspective for so long that hopefully I can give you another and that you are more important to me than any children we may or may not have. *You.*'

Amelia listened, her heart swelling with love for this amazing man. His words were said with total conviction and she knew he believed every single thing he'd said.

'I want to believe you,' she whispered. 'What if you say this now but later on you change your mind?'

'Change my mind about loving you? Never.'

'I meant about the children.'

'No. Not going to happen.'

'How can you be so sure?'

'That's elementary, dear Watson. You mean the world to me. You and Yolanda—you *are* my world. Without you by my side I can't breathe, I can't sleep, I can't function properly. I want you more than I want to have another child, so believe me. Believe that my love for you continues to grow so rapidly it's difficult to control. I've been married before, and what you and I have…is so different. Different from anything I've ever felt and it's right. In fact, it's perfect. You're perfect.' He held her gaze. 'There's only one thing missing.'

'What's that?'

'To hear you say that you love me, too.'

Amelia felt the weight start to lift from her heart. Could this be real? Could this be happening? To her? The man she loved and adored also loved her. He accepted her for who she was, the way she was, and he still loved her! It was a miracle—*her* miracle.

She looked into his rich brown eyes and a smile touched the corners of her lips. 'I do, Harrison. I do love you. I love you so much that my heart is overflowing with the emotion and these past few weeks have been the most miserable of my life.'

'Mine, too.' He smiled at her. 'Let's not do that again.'

'No. Oh, but what about England? We'll need to be separated when I—'

'Nope. Not going to happen.'

'What? What do you mean?'

'I mean, Dr Watson, that we have a lot of work to do in the coming weeks.'

'We do?'

'Yes, because Yolanda and I are going to accompany you back to England. We're going to stay with you, help you study and pass your exams with flying colours. Then we're going to pack up your belongings and shift everything back here to Australia—back here where you belong.'

'Oh, are we? Do I even get consulted in this?'

For the first time Harrison felt uncertain. Was he going too far, too fast? 'Well?' He swallowed and waited. 'Do you think it's a good idea?'

Amelia glanced down at Yolanda, playing happily on the floor, before looking back at the man she adored. She'd been running for so long, hiding herself away, trying not to get involved in relationships in case they ended in heartbreak. Not this one. No. Harrison had shown her, would continue to show her for the rest of her life that she was important to him. She felt it, she needed it…she needed him. He understood… somehow… He understood about her fertility problems and he was saying he didn't care. She wanted to be with him, to be a mother to Yolanda more than anything. No more running. 'I think it sounds perfect.'

Harrison breathed out with relief. 'Whew. You had me worried there for a second.'

'And when we return to Australia? What do I do then?'

'Work here in the hospital.'

'You're offering me a job?'

'Yes. You're a brilliant doctor, AJ.'

'OK. I accept—the job.'

'And the marriage proposal?'

Amelia glanced down to find Yolanda staring up at them both. 'Well, I don't think it's totally my decision.' She beckoned to Yolanda and the little girl stood, Harrison letting Amelia go for a second so he could scoop his daughter up. He shifted her to his hip and placed his other arm about Amelia, the three of them forming a family unit.

'Yolanda,' Harrison said, 'would you like Amelia to come and live with us and marry Daddy and be your mummy?'

'My *mummy*?' Yolanda's eyes almost bulged out of her head. '*Yes!* Yes, yes, yes.' Yolanda wriggled from his arms and he let her go, pulling Amelia close again, both of them watching the little girl start jumping around the room, clapping her hands. 'She tan be da mummy and you tan be da daddy and Mrs D. tan be da gwan-ma and I tan be da prwetty gel.'

Harrison's smile increased as he looked from Yolanda to Amelia. 'That sounds perfect. What do you say, my Amelia-Jane?'

'I say…yes.'

Harrison bent to kiss her, knowing he would never tire of holding this woman, of kissing her, of spending every moment he could with her by his side. When he lifted his head, he smiled. 'You be the mummy.' He kissed her luscious mouth again.

'And you be the daddy,' she said, and kissed him back with all the love in her heart.

'We be a family!' Yolanda said with glee, and both adults laughed, knowing she was one hundred per cent right.

EPILOGUE

'CAN you carry this over for me, please?' Amelia asked Yolanda.

'Of course I can.' The six-year-old rolled her eyes and took the bag her mother was holding out to her. 'I'm six now.'

'I know, darling.' Amelia took Yolanda's free hand and shut the door to their house behind her before checking for traffic and walking across the road for breakfast on the beach. Once they reached the sand, Yolanda dropped the bag, broke free and ran to where her father was sitting in the shallows, a baby boy of eight months on his knee.

Amelia picked up the bag Yolanda had dropped and carried it over to the table where Mrs D. was sitting reading a book. 'Right. I think we're almost ready to start breakfast.'

'You'll have to get them out of the water first,' Mrs D. pointed out. 'Little Scott is definitely a water baby.'

Amelia looked down the beach at her family. Scott was indeed a water baby and he'd settled into their family as though he was meant to be there. Overseas adoption hadn't been easy, but finally they'd been blessed with Scott and he was simply the most gorgeous, easygoing baby.

Yolanda had improved dramatically, being part of a two-parent family, and Mrs D. had enjoyed six months of travelling around Europe and staying with Amelia's relatives in the United Kingdom. Of course, she'd rushed home the instant she'd heard the news about Scott, and Amelia had been glad of the surrogate grandmother's help.

'You may as well join them, Amelia. The food will wait.'

'Good idea,' she said, and shed her sarong to reveal her two-piece bathing suit. The scar from her total hysterectomy was hardly noticeable and although the recovery had been long, she was now fitter and healthier than she'd been for most of her life.

Amelia couldn't help smiling as she headed down the beach, feeling happy and free, knowing she was loved for who she was and able to love those closest to her in return. Her life was like a fairy-tale and she was the princess living in the castle with her very own Prince Charming.

'Mum!' Yolanda called, and waved and ran up the beach to meet her. 'Let's sculpt another castle. We need to practise for the next competition. Everyone loved our castle last year.'

'They did, indeed.' Amelia ran her fingers through Yolanda's blonde curls, which were now halfway down her back, before she straightened her hat. Sitting down, she glanced over at Harrison who picked up Scott and brought him over, the baby holding his arms out to her the instant he spotted her.

'There's your mummy,' Harrison said, giving his son a quick kiss before handing him over. 'He's been splashing so happily. He loves the water.'

Amelia smiled. 'Just like his father.'

Harrison leaned over and pressed a kiss to his wife's lips. 'Mmm. I doubt I'll ever tire of kissing you, my Amelia-Jane.'

'Yech.' Yolanda stuck her tongue out. 'I'm never gonna kiss boys when I'm older.'

'Can I have your word on that?' Harrison asked dryly.

'Dig, Dad. I need more sand.' She jumped up, raced up to the table and brought back her bucket. 'Water, Dad.'

'What am I? Your slave?'

Yolanda grinned but sighed dramatically and Amelia smiled. She would make a wonderful actress when she grew up. *'Please*, Dad?'

He took the opportunity to kiss his wife again then headed off to do his daughter's bidding. When he returned, they all sat around. 'What are we building today?' he asked.

'A happily ever after,' Yolanda announced.

Both parents frowned. 'What does that look like?'

'I know,' she replied with confidence, and as her hands squeezed the sand, she laughed with joy and they realised she *did* know.

0107 Gen Std HB

MILLS & BOON®

Live the emotion

FEBRUARY 2007 HARDBACK TITLES

ROMANCE™

The Marriage Possession *Helen Bianchin* 978 0 263 19572 9
The Sheikh's Unwilling Wife *Sharon Kendrick* 978 0 263 19573 6
The Italian's Inexperienced Mistress *Lynne Graham*
    978 0 263 19574 3
The Sicilian's Virgin Bride *Sarah Morgan* 978 0 263 19575 0
The Rich Man's Bride *Catherine George* 978 0 263 19576 7
Wife by Contract, Mistress by Demand *Carole Mortimer*
    978 0 263 19577 4
Wife by Approval *Lee Wilkinson* 978 0 263 19578 1
The Sheikh's Ransomed Bride *Annie West* 978 0 263 19579 8
Raising the Rancher's Family *Patricia Thayer* 978 0 263 19580 4
Matrimony with His Majesty *Rebecca Winters* 978 0 263 19581 1
In the Heart of the Outback... *Barbara Hannay* 978 0 263 19582 8
Rescued: Mother-To-Be *Trish Wylie* 978 0 263 19583 5
The Sheikh's Reluctant Bride *Teresa Southwick*
    978 0 263 19584 2
Marriage for Baby *Melissa McClone* 978 0 263 19585 9
City Doctor, Country Bride *Abigail Gordon* 978 0 263 19586 6
The Emergency Doctor's Daughter *Lucy Clark* 978 0 263 19587 3

HISTORICAL ROMANCE™

A Most Unconventional Courtship *Louise Allen* 978 0 263 19751 8
A Worthy Gentleman *Anne Herries* 978 0 263 19752 5
Sold and Seduced *Michelle Styles* 978 0 263 19753 2

MEDICAL ROMANCE™

His Very Own Wife and Child *Caroline Anderson*
    978 0 263 19788 4
The Consultant's New-Found Family *Kate Hardy*
    978 0 263 19789 1
A Child to Care For *Dianne Drake* 978 0 263 19790 7
His Pregnant Nurse *Laura Iding* 978 0 263 19791 4

MILLS & BOON®

0107 Gen Std LP

Live the emotion

FEBRUARY 2007 LARGE PRINT TITLES

ROMANCE™

Title	ISBN
Purchased by the Billionaire *Helen Bianchin*	978 0 263 19423 4
Master of Pleasure *Penny Jordan*	978 0 263 19424 1
The Sultan's Virgin Bride *Sarah Morgan*	978 0 263 19425 8
Wanted: Mistress and Mother *Carol Marinelli*	978 0 263 19426 5
Promise of a Family *Jessica Steele*	978 0 263 19427 2
Wanted: Outback Wife *Ally Blake*	978 0 263 19428 9
Business Arrangement Bride *Jessica Hart*	978 0 263 19429 6
Long-Lost Father *Melissa James*	978 0 263 19430 2

HISTORICAL ROMANCE™

Title	ISBN
Mistaken Mistress *Margaret McPhee*	978 0 263 19382 4
The Inconvenient Duchess *Christine Merrill*	978 0 263 19383 1
Falcon's Desire *Denise Lynn*	978 0 263 19384 8

MEDICAL ROMANCE™

Title	ISBN
The Sicilian Doctor's Proposal *Sarah Morgan*	978 0 263 19335 0
The Firefighter's Fiancé *Kate Hardy*	978 0 263 19336 7
Emergency Baby *Alison Roberts*	978 0 263 19337 4
In His Special Care *Lucy Clark*	978 0 263 19338 1
Bride at Bay Hospital *Meredith Webber*	978 0 263 19533 0
The Flight Doctor's Engagement *Laura Iding*	978 0 263 19534 7

MILLS & BOON®

Live the emotion

MARCH 2007 HARDBACK TITLES

ROMANCE™

The Billionaire's Scandalous Marriage *Emma Darcy*
978 0 263 19588 0
The Desert King's Virgin Bride *Sharon Kendrick*
978 0 263 19589 7
Aristides' Convenient Wife *Jacqueline Baird* 978 0 263 19590 3
The Pregnancy Affair *Anne Mather* 978 0 263 19591 0
Bought for Her Baby *Melanie Milburne* 978 0 263 19592 7
The Australian's Housekeeper Bride *Lindsay Armstrong*
978 0 263 19593 4
The Brazilian's Blackmail Bargain *Abby Green* 978 0 263 19594 1
The Greek Millionaire's Mistress *Catherine Spencer*
978 0 263 19595 8
The Sheriff's Pregnant Wife *Patricia Thayer* 978 0 263 19596 5
The Prince's Outback Bride *Marion Lennox* 978 0 263 19597 2
The Secret Life of Lady Gabriella *Liz Fielding* 978 0 263 19598 9
Back to Mr & Mrs *Shirley Jump* 978 0 263 19599 6
Memo: Marry Me? *Jennie Adams* 978 0 263 19600 9
Hired by the Cowboy *Donna Alward* 978 0 263 19601 6
Dr Constantine's Bride *Jennifer Taylor* 978 0 263 19602 3
Emergency at Riverside Hospital *Joanna Neil* 978 0 263 19603 0

HISTORICAL ROMANCE™

The Wicked Earl *Margaret McPhee* 978 0 263 19754 9
Working Man, Society Bride *Mary Nichols* 978 0 263 19755 6
Traitor or Temptress *Helen Dickson* 978 0 263 19756 3

MEDICAL ROMANCE™

A Bride for Glenmore *Sarah Morgan* 978 0 263 19792 1
A Marriage Meant To Be *Josie Metcalfe* 978 0 263 19793 8
His Runaway Nurse *Meredith Webber* 978 0 263 19794 5
The Rescue Doctor's Baby Miracle *Dianne Drake*
978 0 263 19795 2

MILLS & BOON®

Live the emotion

0207 Gen Std LP

MARCH 2007 LARGE PRINT TITLES

ROMANCE™

Purchased for Revenge *Julia James*	978 0 263 19431 9
The Playboy Boss's Chosen Bride *Emma Darcy*	
	978 0 263 19432 6
Hollywood Husband, Contract Wife *Jane Porter*	
	978 0 263 19433 3
Bedded by the Desert King *Susan Stephens*	978 0 263 19434 0
Her Christmas Wedding Wish *Judy Christenberry*	
	978 0 263 19435 7
Married Under the Mistletoe *Linda Goodnight*	978 0 263 19436 4
Snowbound Reunion *Barbara McMahon*	978 0 263 19437 1
The Tycoon's Instant Family *Caroline Anderson*	
	978 0 263 19438 8

HISTORICAL ROMANCE™

A Lady of Rare Quality *Anne Ashley*	978 0 263 19385 5
Talk of the Ton *Mary Nichols*	978 0 263 19386 2
The Norman's Bride *Terri Brisbin*	978 0 263 19387 9

MEDICAL ROMANCE™

Caring for His Child *Amy Andrews*	978 0 263 19339 8
The Surgeon's Special Gift *Fiona McArthur*	978 0 263 19340 4
A Doctor Beyond Compare *Melanie Milburne*	978 0 263 19341 1
Rescued By Marriage *Dianne Drake*	978 0 263 19342 8
The Nurse's Longed-For Family *Fiona Lowe*	978 0 263 19535 4
Her Baby's Secret Father *Lynne Marshall*	978 0 263 19536 1

K.M.

N.M.